Lock Down Publications and Ca$h Presents

I0658340

STANDING ON HER BUSINESS

BO$$ BYTCH SHYT

Written By
DG SANTANA

First Edition 2024

Printed in the United States of America

This is a work of fiction. Names, characters, places, and incidents either are products of the author's imagination or are used fictitiously. Any similarity to actual events or locales or persons, living or dead, is entirely coincidental.

Lock Down Publications
P.O. Box 944
Stockbridge, GA 30281
www.lockdownpublications.com

Like our page on Facebook: Lock Down Publications
www.facebook.com/lockdownpublications.ldp

Stay Connected with Us!

Text **LOCKDOWN** to 22828 to stay up-to-date with new releases, sneak peaks, contests and more…

Like our page on Facebook:
Lock Down Publications

Join Lock Down Publications/The New Era Reading Group

Visit our website:
www.lockdownpublications.com

Follow us on Instagram:
Lock Down Publications

Email Us: We want to hear from you!

Chapter 1

Laney laid back on her bed, with her R&B music playing in the background, as she long stroked herself with the muscular plastic dick that she had at her disposal.

"Damn, bitch! Open them legs up just a lil' bit more. I want to see that lil pussy buss all the way open for a nigga." Her other half, Zion, growled from the other side of her phone screen. He laid on his jail bunk and stroked his pulsing erection, imagining that it was him inside of his woman.

His nasty words turned her on even more, and she obeyed his command obediently. He was a hundred miles away and got her rocks off better than her fuck buddy around the corner. She closed her eyes and imagined him balls deep inside of her as her climax rose.

"Uhmmmmm! Daddy, I feel it! I feel it!" She informed sexily while speeding up the strokes.

They both sped their pace up and climaxed together, as if they were actually in each other's arms at the moment.

"I *still* don't understand how that shit feels so real with you. You better not have no spell on a bitch," she warned as she sat up, preparing to clean herself.

Zion just laid back on his bunk in pure bliss, too drained to clean himself at the moment. "Nah, you know I'm scared of them spirits. I'm just deep stroking your soul. That's all."

"Uhmm! Well, keep stroking, nigga. Keep stroking," she encouraged while looking at his sexy, yellow ass sprawled on his bunk.

"And you know I will," he promised before sitting up and looking into his phone that was propped up on the other end of his bed. "I'm about to have to call you back though. I'm late for this meeting. Thank you for the quickie, shawty."

She made a show of doing a childish pout. "Okayyy, and you're welcome... I guess I'll just go ahead and get in the shower. I have a long night ahead of me."

He picked his phone up and brought it closer to his uniquely sculpted, tattooed face. "Handle your business and live your life but I don't give a fuck what's going on out there. Your lil' ass better check in when you can." His voice was soft, but it wasn't gentle, so he meant business.

"I got you, bae," she promised. "I love you, sexy papa!"

"I love you too, sexy mama," he said before blowing her a kiss and ending the call.

She took her iPad off of the kickstand and placed it on her dresser, so it could charge. Then, she stood and sighed deeply. She *really, really* wished that Zion was out to live life with her. Indeed, they made the best out of their situation, but whenever they weren't actually talking, reality was slapping her in the face. His presence was definitely felt, but at the end of the day, he wasn't actually there.

She shook her head rapidly and blinked her eyes a few times. She wasn't about to allow herself to go on the emotional rollercoaster that Zion's ass constantly took her on. She had to prepare herself for the night ahead, so she headed into the bathroom and submerged into her sizable walk-in shower.

****

Laney stood, naked, inside of her walk-in closet, looking in the wall-length mirror on the door to her closet. Her tiny, tattooed body wasn't perfect, but she was definitely a bad bitch in every way.

5

After she was done admiring her pretty brown curves, she started the task of finding the perfect garments to cover them. She settled for a black, Amiri bodysuit, a black, Moncler bubble coat to go over that, and furry Chanel boots to match.

"Girllll, you looking like a whole snack out here! Zion might be in trouble tonight!" Her adopted daughter, Mini, teased from the doorway of her closet.

The naked eye would mistake the pair for mother and daughter since they resembled each other so much. Then, there was the fact that Laney was far too young to actually be Mini's mother, but they still played the role despite the critics. *Nobody* could tell them they didn't share the same genes.

"Girl, Trey Songz could walk into my office, drop down onto one knee, and propose to a bitch, and Zion *still* wouldn't be in trouble. That's my soulmate no matter what or who!" Laney informed matter-of-factly.

Mini placed a gentle hand on her chest while batting her chinky eyes. "Awww! Y'all two are the cutest. I wish they'd just let the nigga out already. He still being punished for a mistake he made when he was young as hell. I know he learned his lesson by now."

Laney sighed, grabbed one of her Chanel purses, and made her way toward Mini. "Come on. I got to go. Stay out of my shit and keep that little boy out of my shit please. If you want to fuck him, do it somewhere else. This ain't no damn hotel." She purposely changed the subject while escorting Mini out of her bedroom.

"Don't do me!" Mini shouted before rolling her eyes and stomping into her room without a care in the entire world.

Laney sighed again as she watched her little protégé strut down the hall with her little booty jiggling all over the place. Nine times out of ten, she'd end up being even more of a handful than Laney, and that wasn't necessarily a good thing.

She'd have to find her a Zion to put up with her needy and moody ass.

"Let's see what Charlotte's nightlife has in store tonight," she said to herself before putting on her Chanel shades and exiting her condo-suite in the Uptown area of the city.

Chapter 2

Superior Static Lounge was an elegant cocktail bar and lounge in Second Ward. It was one of the places to be in the city, and she prided herself on being the manager of the supreme establishment. Sometimes, she still found it hard to believe how far she'd come from the rusty stripper pole she used to swing on.

Her personal security guard, Lester, parked her grey Maserati in her reserved parking space outside of her establishment. She shook her head at the line that was building out front. She made her way toward the entrance with Lester hot on her heels. He was like her own personal guard dog, and he went *everywhere* with her.

"Dave, you dead ass wrong for making these people wait out here in this cold ass weather like this," she chastised once they made it to the entrance.

Dave was head-of-security over the lounge, and he took his job a little too serious. He was the more muscle than brains type. "What?! We got too many people in there already. They'll just be in there standing around and shit. This a five-star lounge, not a local club."

"So!" Laney shrugged her shoulders with a slight mug. "Get these people inside before they decide to spend their time and money somewhere else. This muthafucka gone be jumping like a club tonight!" she warned before storming past him into the establishment.

8

The place was jumping though, and it was just an ordinary Wednesday night. For the last year or so, it had been like this — every single day of the week. Static cashed out on a few A-list entertainers to super-promote his establishment, and it was history from there. That move set him up for life. It was one of the dopest investments Laney had ever seen a person make. Static was her big homie and the reason she was currently in her current position. He had kept it a thousand with her since day one, and for that, he had her loyalty and service for life. She put him above everyone, except for Mini and Zion.

"Uhmm, Boss Lady, that crazy dude with the lazy eye is in your office waiting for you. He been here for twenty minutes already," Drina casually slid up on her and informed. She was Laney's favorite bottle girl and kept a watchful eye out on things when she wasn't around.

"Who, J-Rock? What the fuck he want?" she asked urgently.

Drina shrugged her slim shoulders. "I don't know, but the nigga *did not* look happy at all. I'm surprised Dave ain't say nothing about it. Security just let the nigga walk into your shit."

"Yeah, unfortunately, he's a VIP member and probably told Dave not to tell me, so he could surprise me... Thanks for the heads up, girl. Swing by the office a lil' later on. I'm going to take care of you," Laney said before making her way through the main floor toward her upstairs office.

"Please make this quick. I have a lot of business to tend to tonight," she spat as soon as she walked into the office casually and unfazed by his brooding presence.

J-Rock laid back comfortably on her miniature couch, staring up at her. His guard dog stood beside him, staring at her guard dog.

"Stop eye fucking me and state your business, J-Rock! I swear I don't got time for your bullshit tonight! You already

9

violating by walking up in my shit unannounced," she spat with a little more force than before.

"No, yo' lil' bitty ass is in violation. One of *your* hoes stole a lot of money and product from one of my lil' homies, and I'm here to decide if you put her up to it. You train and groom every one of them bitches." He pointed out accusingly.

Laney finally took a seat in her chair behind her desk and noticeably processed the news. "Wait, what? I'm lost. One of *your* lil' homies was dumb enough to expose a whole gold digger to that kind of treasure, and you're sitting right there, trying to blame *me* for something most of the bitches in this fucking city would've done? Come on now, J. Make it make sense. You're not the brightest bulb in the ceiling, but I gave you more credit than this." She was extra on the sassiness.

J-Rock laid there a little while more and eye fucked her some more before slowly standing up to his full 6'4" length. "If I find out you had something to do with this, Static's not going to be able to stop me from the shit I got in store for you and that lil' fine ass daughter of yours," he threatened before letting himself out of the office with his shooter in tow.

"He's definitely going to be a problem." Lester predicted while standing there looking like a rugged version of Jamie Foxx in his late thirties.

Laney gave him a knowing look while taking off her coat. "No, he already is a damn problem. In more ways than one, which is why the muthafucker has to be stopped. Now, I need you to go handle something for me."

"What's that?"

"Go to the Holiday Inn by the airport and pick lil' shorty up. Keep all the product and let her keep half of the money. Then, I need you to drive her up to NYC personally. She'll have to lay low up there until I can get J-Rock out of the way."

"New York? Shouldn't she go somewhere a little slower to lay low?" he asked.

"Have you seen her? She'll stick out like a sore thumb in a country town. She's a City Girl, and plus, I have connections out there who has work for her."

"That's understandable, but I don't feel comfortable leaving you alone for that long. It's too dangerous out here right now, and with J-Rock on your trail, it doesn't seem right," he admitted seriously.

Laney showed her charming smile. Lester's obsession with her safety was adorable. She helped him sober up off of the alcohol, gave him a purpose after the Marines had kicked him to the curb, so he devoted himself to her like he used to be devoted to his country. Plus, she paid way better than Uncle Sam. He had every reason to be overprotective over her.

"I'll be fine," she assured with a wave of a manicured hand. "I'll get Dave to take me home. Plus, I don't plan on going anywhere until you get back anyway."

Lester rubbed his bald, walnut-shaped head then let his hand run down to his thick beard. He was doing calculations in his head. "Alright, man. Try to keep your promise and stay your ass in the condo until I get back."

"It wasn't a promise, but I will," she stated in the midst of mild laughter. "Go ahead and get it done. Don't forget to stash those drugs somewhere for me before you drive up there. I'll figure out what to do with them while you're gone."

"I probably could help with that. I'll hit my cousin in the Chi," he offered.

She thought on it for a second then nodded. "We'll discuss it when you return."

He nodded back and disappeared.

"Wheewww!" She released a deep sigh once he was alone.

She was under a lot of pressure at the moment, being the underdog and all, but the underestimation only fueled her

11

determination. One day soon, she'd be able to breathe easy and just focus on building stronger relationships with Zion and Mini. It was all she thought about, but for now, she had to do the best she could with the hand she was dealt.

Chapter 3

The night was still young for Laney, but she was tired already. She sat at her desk, eyeing the many camera feeds that showed up on one of the two big computer screens that sat on her desk.

"I'm surprised this bitch throat ain't swollen yet. He been fucking her face for a lil' while now. He need to hurry up and get off, so his weird ass can get up out of here." She observed audibly.

There were four explicit VIP rooms in the basement for elite members only. Laney was the woman to come to if you were looking for a quality nut. All of her girls were highly addictive in one way or another, and that was how she maintained her reputation of being the *Queen of Pleasure*. That was what people were calling her these days but if they only knew how much pain she was really capable of.

The cameras were set up in the boom-boom-rooms just in case the need for blackmail ever arose. She ran the idea of opportunity across Static a few months back, and he greenlighted it. Laney knew that the key was to remain an asset, and she was doing a good job of it. If everything went how she had it planned, she'd be set for life herself pretty soon.

She broke her attention away from the monitors and stood up, so she could walk over to her super-sized tinted window that overlooked the lounge. She didn't own the place, but she ran it, and it was her queendome. She felt proud watching the smooth operation unfold beneath her, and she took pride in all of her girls. She wouldn't be who she was without them. Pussy was power, and she had the best pussy in the city in her palm.

A call popped up on her iPhone watch. It was Zion. She rolled her eyes with a smile before answering the call. "Yesss, Daddy!"

"Don't 'yes, daddy' me! Where the fuck you been at?" he asked grimly.

"Don't start your shit, nigga. I only been gone for a few hours, and I was about to call you soon anyway, so don't do me," she informed defensively.

"A few hours too damn long. You know I be missing you, woman," he retorted sweetly.

"You so damn bipolar." She blushed. "I miss you too, you damn sour patch. What you got going on over there?"

"In the lab, handling this business. I'm really tied up right now, just wanted to hear your voice and say I love you before I put my phone on airplane mode."

"Your ass be busier than me in there. Well, I'm glad you're making the time count and doing something with yourself, bae. I love you too though and will be on your bumper as soon as I wake up so make sure you take that phone off airplane mode before you take it in."

He chuckled. "Don't be on my muthafuckin' bumper. Fuck wrong with you, shawty? Nah, I got you though. Goodnight, beautiful," he said before ending the call.

She released her usual sigh whenever she departed from him. It was like she lost a piece of herself every time he left her. She quickly pushed those emotions aside and got back in her boss bitch zone. She had just spotted somebody on the floor that she needed to have a little chat with.

She descended from her throne and hit the floor. Per usual, she was acknowledged and shown love when she was seen. The handsome chocolate man she was there for sat comfortably on one of the many couches that sat strategically throughout the establishment. Two of Laney's best floor girls sat on each side of him, keeping him entertained.

Laney waved her hand, and the girls got up without a second thought. Laney took a seat next to the handsome man and crossed her little legs. "I hope you're enjoying all this free pussy I'm providing."

"Of course I am, and that's good news for you because as long as the pussy's good, you'll continue to receive a discount for the services I'm providing," he countered smugly with a smile to match.

The handsome man went by Tyreese Manning. He was her criminal defense attorney and one of the most important pieces on her chessboard, so she couldn't even dispute that. "Whatever... Tell me something good please. I need some good news, man."

"Ahhhhhh... You're a good paying customer, and I respect your mind, so I'm going to give it to you raw and not even going to bullshit with you. That man, J-Rock, is a fucking problem. And I don't mean that mildly. If Static can't put a leash on him quick, he's going to sink your entire ship. And that I can guarantee." His tone and expression were serious.

"So, they're getting somewhere with the investigation?" she asked with butterflies in her stomach.

"I mean, my source won't share specifics, but they did let me know that J-Rock is definitely the reason why you're all under the microscope now. He's definitely a powerful force to be dealt with, and that makes him a perfect target for the government to make an example out of."

Laney probably released her hundredth sigh for the week already. She was so over the constant complications. "Damn, man. I don't have time for this shit. It's already enough to worry about without the fucking Feds breathing down our backs."

"Well, I suggest you come up with a plan fast because as long as J-Rock's in the picture, you're a target. Plus, you having private meetings with him in your office doesn't help either. They're watching his *every* move," he assured matter-of-factly.

She cut her eyes at him. "You was here when I came in? I didn't see you."

"Nah, I had caught him coming out."

She nodded her head. "Alright. Just see if your source will accept extra payment to throw in some details," she instructed before standing up and making her rounds.

Chapter 4

The doors to the lounge officially closed at two o'clock. Laney usually left them open for special members, but tonight, she really shut shit down at two. Only Dave and herself stayed behind. Manning had her spooked with the whole investigation business. She had to pump her brakes and switch her entire operation up now – all because of J-Rock's ole reckless ass.

"Fuckkkk!" she spat irritably.

Dave gave her a knowing look. "Trouble in paradise, huh?" He sat on a bar stool a few feet away from the couch that she sat on.

"What you think, Genius? While you over there smirking and shit, my problems are your problems," she reminded unpleasantly. "I'm over here trying to complete the impossible, and you're over there drinking like it's something to fucking celebrate."

Dave put his drink down and quickly raised his sausage fingers in surrender. "Damn, girl! I was just shooting the shit like I always do. I ain't know it was that bad. I mean, J-Rock popping up out of nowhere was weird, but I ain't know we was in crisis mode."

"J-Rock is the fucking crisis! That's what I'm saying. There's no way I'm the only person who sees the shit," she stressed with much enthusiasm.

Dave dropped his hands and picked his drink back up. "Shit, J-Rock been chilling lately. What's the problem?"

Laney rolled her eyes and threw her hands up. "That's fear talking right there. If you was looking at the shit from a clear mind, that same blinding fear is what he uses to manipulate other people to actually want to do his fucked-up deeds. Or in this case, turn a blind eye to them."

"Watch it now, woman. I fear no man!" He countered defensively while shooting her a stern stare.

"I'm just saying," she informed in a softer tone. "All men say that they don't fear nobody, but if you don't fear a nigga like J-Rock, you're either as evil as he is or you're just plain stupid, and I don't take you for either."

"Where's all this shit coming from anyway? You acting like he's not on our side or something. He don't pose us no threats. He provide you the same protection in the streets that I provide in this lounge. What's the problem?"

Laney sighed. She didn't want to lay all her cards on the table with him. The truth was that she didn't feel that she could fully trust him, even though he was up under her umbrella. For all she knew, he probably reported to J-Rock too on the sly. "Just forget it. I told his ass not to be popping up in here, and that's what the hell he better do! Come on. I'm ready to go home," she spat before getting up, grabbing her jacket, and heading out of the building.

****

Laney walked in on Mini doing a live video for all one hundred eighty thousand of her followers. She was an Instagram model, and she even surprised Laney with some of the celebrities that followed her. She was even verified with a blue check on her page. It solidified her position as a public figure. She took advantage of her opportunities, just like Laney had taught her, but she went an extra mile when she started an OnlyFans page against Laney's wishes.

Laney had stopped talking to Mini for a whole month after that, but when she saw the type of money Mini was

STANDING ON HER BUSINESS | DG SANTANA

bringing in, she had no choice but to respect it. She had started stripping when she was seventeen, and Mini starting an OnlyFans page was basically the same thing. They were just showing themselves off but never got touched. The only difference was that Mini was making five times as much as Laney did when she was stripping, and that was saying *a lot*.

"I got to talk to my mama, y'all! I'll probably be back on here before the sun comes up and do a lil' dancing for y'all or something," she informed before blowing a kiss into her phone camera and ending the live video. "How you come home early looking tired?" she asked Laney just as she plopped down on the couch with a sigh.

"I don't even want to talk about my night... What you need to talk to me about? You pregnant, bitch?" She looked at Mini with a raised brow.

Mini laughed. "Oh-M-Gee! For the millionth time, noooo! I'm on birth control, damnnnn! Nah, but it's about my boyfriend."

"What about him?" Laney asked with a raised brow.

"You know he be trapping and whatnot. Well, his plug just got locked up, and he needs a new connect. You know I only deal with legit people, so I was just wonderinggggg..."

"What? Oh, hellll no! That lil' nigga probably the one that told on his plug in the first place. I hope you ain't been telling that boy my business either!" Concern was clear on Laney's face.

Mini rolled her eyes. "Ma, don't be like that. He just needs a lil' help."

"All I got for him is some advice... Quit while he's ahead. And that goes for whatever side of the law he's on. Now, if he wants a job, I'll point him in the right direction, but anything outside of that, he's going to have to hit the pavement." She made that clear before getting up and heading to her bedroom.

She was tired and had a long day ahead of her tomorrow. So, she showered and called Zion. He answered groggily,

19

halfway asleep. They only said a few words to one another before they both fell asleep on the phone together as if they shared the same bed.

Chapter 5

Laney woke up the next afternoon and checked her phone. Zion wasn't on the line, but he left a few messages wishing her a prosperous day and promising to check in with her as soon as possible. She sent a cute voice message back to him then gave Lester a call.

"What's up, lil' sis?" he answered.

"Everything go smooth with her?"

"Yeah," he assured evenly. "I dropped her off with your peoples, now I'm on my way back. I'll be there in about five hours."

Laney nodded, even though he couldn't see her. "Get some sleep when you get back. I won't be leaving out until late. Be here by twelve."

"Roger that," he confirmed before ending the call.

Laney got up, brushed her teeth, then headed into the kitchen, so she could make breakfast for the house. As she prepared the meal, her mind raced a thousand miles per minute, trying to fixate a master plan that landed her on top. Making it out of this storm wasn't an option for her. She'd worked too damn hard to get where she was to let someone else tarnish her legacy.

She was whipping egg yolk in a big bowl when her eyes lit up like a brand-new dope fiend. A dope plan had just come to her head, and it brought a literal smile to her face because if it worked, the storm would be over just that fast. The only problem was that the plan wouldn't be easy, so she had to figure out what angle she wanted to approach it from.

She cooked the rest of the breakfast on autopilot, preoccupied with her thoughts, plans, and scenarios she drew up in her head. Tonight could possibly be the first night where she got a good, peaceful night's sleep in a *longgg time*.

****

Later on that night, after catching up on sleep and spending quality time with Zion and Mini, Laney was ready to hit the streets. She'd been living the nightlife so long that she'd become a night owl. She lived a vampire's life and had no complaints about it. It was literally a part of her now. She got dressed and headed out, meeting Lester in the parking garage of her building.

"Brotherrrrr!" she greeted in exaggeration as she made her way to him.

All that could be heard in the garage was a strong engine revving in the distance and the sound of her Prada heels clanking on the smooth concrete floor.

"What's up, lil' sis?" he greeted just before she made it into his arms.

They hugged, and he opened the back door of her truck for her, so she could hop in. "Alright. We got a stop to make before we get to the lounge," she informed.

"Where to?" he asked after getting behind the wheel and starting the engine.

"That lot that Static had just bought not too long ago."

He glanced at her through the rearview mirror. "Where they're building the apartment complex? What the hell you need to go out there for?"

"Just drive," she instructed impatiently. "Going to make a bitch late for her meeting."

About thirty minutes later, they were pulling up into the vacant lot. "Looks like you're late for your meeting anyway," Lester teased.

"No, this muthafucker is just early. With his paranoid ass... Stay in the car. I'll be right back," she spat before hopping out of the car and making her way up to the Escalade that faced them.

A tall, handsome, and muscular man waited in front of a black Jaguar SUV with his arms crossed as he peered down at her through his dark grey eyes. His name was Murk. His 6'2" frame towered over her 4'11" height, but she met his gaze with the same intense glare. She was unfazed by his intimidating nature. He was a certified predator in the streets, but she didn't care about all of that.

"What the hell you call me out here for? In the middle of the night at that," he asked curiously.

"I called you out here because I know personally that you're a smart man, so you need to make the smart decision."

He gave her a confused look. "Just say what you got to say, woman. I don't got time for no riddles."

"You need to kill J-Rock and take over Rock Nation," she spat matter-of-factly with a hand on her hip.

"What?!" Murk said while looking around cautiously. "Girl, what the fuck is you talking about?" All of his senses had just heightened that fast. He was a naturally nonchalant type of person, who didn't rattle easily, but a statement like that was enough to rattle anyone who knew J-Rock.

"You heard me, nigga. It's just me and you out here, so you don't have to play dumb like it's not something you haven't thought about before."

Murk stood there, staring at her suspiciously through squinted eyes. If she would've been anyone else, he would've pulled out his pistol and threatened their lives for suggesting and accusing him of such a thing. J-Rock was literally the only person that he knew who was way more paranoid than himself, and he wasn't above pulling a stunt like this to test Murk's loyalty. He'd done it before, but Murk knew Laney's heart because they used to be lovers many years ago, and he knew she wouldn't play with his life like that. So, that only meant one thing. She was dead serious, and that kind of scared him.

"Where is all this shit coming from, Ney Ney?" he asked curiously.

"They just launched a federal investigation on Rock Nation, and I fall under that category. I'm not about to go down because of J-Rock's reckless ass, Murk, and I'm sure you're not trying to go down either. So, you need to do what needs to be done," she stated very seriously. She maintained intense eye contact with him just so he would know how serious she was.

He ran a hand down his face and sighed. "You do remember how I ended up being his righthand man in the first place, right? Not one but two niggas before me tried to take him out for his spot. And you know why it didn't work, right? Because the nigga's wayyy fuckin' smarter than the world gives him credit for."

"And you're smarter than J-Rock gives you credit for," she reminded. "You can use that underestimation to your advantage and take the nigga out. I'm telling you, Murk. The government is scared of that man. Rock Nation is getting too big, and they're looking to cut the head off the snake."

Murk shrugged his shoulders obviously. "There's the answer to all of your questions right there."

"Actually, it's not. That is the problem... High ranking people like me and you will take that fall with him."

"Listen here, girl... I'm not going to do no shit like that, and that's the end of the story. Well, that scenario anyway." He took a step closer, so she would hear his next words very clearly. "And watch who you confide in with that lil' plan of yours because J-Rock's fear runs deeper than you think. Everybody don't got love for you like me, Ney Ney. A muthafucka will turn you in just to get on J-Rock's good side."

Laney huffed in agitation. "Whatever... When you end up in that jail cell, and your daughter write you letters asking why you left her for so long, make sure you tell her it's because you was too damn scared to do what needed to be done in order to stay in her life," she spat hurtfully before storming back to her truck where Lester stood outside, waiting for her patiently.

Chapter 6

Laney leaned back in her reclined chair, behind her office desk, at her lounge. Murk had her heated because she knew he wanted to do it. She really saw it in his eyes, but she also saw the fear too. He was scared to do it. J-Rock had the fear of fucking God in everyone he knew, except for Static and herself. At least that was what it seemed like.

His reign of terror began when he was fourteen. He killed his stepfather for drinking the last of the milk in the fridge. He did a few years in juvenile, and once he was out, that was when he started Rock Nation. It started off as a small extortion enterprise, consisting of him and a handful of other hardbody teenagers who looked up to him. Now, Rock Nation was the largest organization in the city of Charlotte. Their hands were in everything from drugs to prostitution, and it consisted of hundreds of ruthless individuals who would kill or die in the name of J-Rock without a second thought.

Laney was taking all of that into account as she assessed the situation at hand. She was coming to the conclusion that she had to approach the battle from another angle. It was obvious that she wouldn't beat him in a toe-to-toe fight, so she had to stop thinking like a nigga and start thinking like a bitch. She was the Queen of Pleasure, and she had to use that to her advantage.

It was right then that another executable plan popped up into her head. She literally popped up out of her seat unconsciously. Once she noticed, she was about to sit back down and work out the details but immediately decided against it. She would work out the details on the way. There was no time to waste.

She grabbed Lester and headed downstairs after locking her office up. She was about to go through the front and hop in her Maserati until she remembered that someone would probably be keeping tabs on her, so she went through the back and asked the head cook for his car keys. He didn't hesitate or ask any questions. He just dug into his pocket and fished out the keys to his new black 2018 Chevy pickup, happy to be able to do a favor for the boss lady.

She thanked him and handed the keys to Lester as they slipped out of the back door. It was raining outside, so they rushed into the truck and were on their way. Laney instructed him to head to Myers Park. It was the wealthiest neighborhood in all of Charlotte. Laney was going to pay someone a surprise visit, and she just prayed that she hit the ball with this swing.

As she looked out the tinted passenger's window at the city veiled in rain, her phone lit up, and Zion's face popped up. He was calling, but she let it ring out. She had too much going on in her head at the moment. As much as she loved his ass, she didn't need him diverting her focus. She was mentally dotting all of her i's and crossing all of her t's.

****

Like Laney, Ta'Jae was a beautiful, brown, successful woman. She was a real boss bitch in her own right. They shared two separate pasts, but they both ended up on the same journey. They were just in two different lanes. Like Laney, Ta'Jae found then groomed young girls and raised them into grown women. The only difference between the two were location and clientele.

Ta'Jae operated in a castle that was set up like a compound for privacy and safety. It was one of the largest estates in Myers Park. It was one of the top three most expensive, hands-down. It was the perfect location for her clientele, which consisted of mostly business moguls and politicians, unlike Laney, who mostly provided services for high-end drug dealers and entertainers. They were in two different lanes and weren't stepping on each other's toes. That meant they weren't competition, which was why Laney was on her way to Ta'Jae's palace.

The streets had officially proclaimed Laney the Queen of Pleasure. Between the lounge, Mini, and her celebrity friends, it was no secret. Laney was notorious in Queen City and clearly had more fame than Ta'Jae, but it was clear that Ta'Jae cashed the bigger bucks. A few months ago, Ta'Jae took it upon herself to nickname herself Goddess of Pleasure on Instagram. Laney normally kept tabs on Ta'Jae's page, since they followed each other, so she caught it. It was cute to her. Although they never actually spoke or acknowledged each other, she felt as if they were connected in a way. Tonight would tell if that was true or not.

In her earlier years of moving to Charlotte, when she still worked at the strip club, she used to spend a lot of her free time just driving around Myers Park, just admiring the elegant neighborhood and all the breathtaking mansions. It was motivational for her. She would envision herself living in the homes, and it comforted her, as if her future was destined to end in this very neighborhood.

That was how she knew exactly where Ta'Jae lived. She posted pictures in front of her house all the time, and that was what originally made Laney follow her in the first place. It was one of her favorite mansions in Myers Park. It was a little far off from the main road, so she would sometimes have to use binoculars just to admire the property back in the day.

"Is this the place?" Lester asked awkwardly. Laney just gave him directions but not the plan. He didn't know why they were out there because it definitely wasn't one of her usual stops. "They're tight on security, I see," he noted as two heavily armed white men approach their truck as they rolled to a stop in front of the main outer gate.

"Yeah, it's not so much security during the day though," she answered then informed.

"Name?" the smallest of the two guards asked cautiously after Lester's window was rolled down.

Lester didn't say a word. He just pointed an index finger at Laney. "I'm Laney from Static Lounge. Tell Ta'Jae I'm here to see her... I don't have an appointment or anything, but I'm sure she'll see me."

A flash of recognition flashed over the guard as his face lit up a little. "Hey, I've heard of you and that lounge. Me and my buddy actually are making plans to visit soon with the wives... She usually doesn't see people who aren't on the list, but I'll call up and tell her you're out here."

Laney loved the fact that her name held weight in high places. She used to envision that too, and it was still sort of unreal how the shit had come true.

"What's all this about?" Lester asked while looking at her with a raised brow.

"You'll see," Laney assured as the guard made his way back to the truck.

"She's waiting on you inside," he informed. "Just drive down this main road until you reach the palace, and her assistant will escort you from there."

Chapter 7

The estate was well lit, and the palace was even more beautiful up close. Laney made a good show of not being googly eyed. She seemed unfazed, like she frequented places like this all the time, but on the inside, she was sucking it all in and observing *every* single detail.

A tall, well-dressed, pecan colored woman approached them as they climbed the stairs of the palace. "Good evening, you two. I'm Yvonne. You must be Laney of course, and you are..." she asked with mild interest.

"I'm Lester, her bodyguard," he answered in his sexy voice before shaking her hand gently.

Laney rolled her eyes with a half-smile. "This place is wonderful."

"Yes, it is. After a year, I'm still not fully used to it," she admitted before turning around and leading the way. "Please follow me."

The palace was even more spectacular on the inside and was even bigger than it looked on the outside. A skinny, white woman with long, blonde hair walked toward them. Laney could tell that she was one of Ta'Jae's girls from the dress she wore to the way she carried herself. She was a certified seductress. That was another thing that set Laney and Ta'Jae apart. Laney mostly had different shades of Black women working for her, but Ta'Jae mostly had white and foreign women who were literally from overseas.

Yvonne stopped the white woman and instructed her to bring Laney to Ta'Jae before assuring Laney that she'd take good care of Lester. Laney pictured the pair together and smiled because they would look cute together. She gave Lester a knowing look before following the snow bunny through the palace.

She followed the snow bunny upstairs and through the maze of a hallway. They ended up in front of a bedroom door that the snow bunny knocked on and walked away, leaving Laney standing there alone.

"Come in!" Ta'Jae instructed from the other side of the door.

Laney took a deep breath and walked into the room. To her surprise, the room looked like a giant damn doll playhouse. It was her four-year-old daughter's room. Laney had seen the little girl on Ta'Jae's Instagram page. She was even more adorable in person than she was in the pictures. She was just a little darker than Ta'Jae, but her skin glowed. She was yapping off at the mouth, how most four-year-old girls did to their moms. Ta'Jae laid with her, trying to get her to fall back to sleep.

Ta'Jae motioned for the nanny to step in for her before standing up and walking toward Laney. She wore a stylish pantsuit without the jacket, and even without the heels, she was several inches taller than Laney. Other than that, they could pass for sisters, especially with the way they slayed their long and wavy wigs. "Girl, you know you wearing that damn coat," she admitted, referring to Laney's purple and white, plaid patchwork, ADEAM, trench coat.

"Appreciate that, girl." Laney thanked her while looking down at her own threads. "My daughter had bought it for me as a Christmas gift."

Ta'Jae nodded. "That little Mini is something else. I follow her as well. She's going places in this life for sure."

"So, you have been paying attention?" Laney asked with a raised brow of interest.

Ta'Jae nodded her head once again. "Follow me... Let's head to my office."

She blew her baby girl an air kiss before exiting the room and leading the way through the complex hallway structure. The house had to be renovated a few times because there was no way it was originally built like that. It looked purposely designed for it to be difficult to navigate.

Ta'Jae stopped abruptly in the middle of the hallway where she pushed the wall. It opened like a door into her plush hidden office. Laney couldn't hide her amazement of that. "Nahhh! Not the hidden office though. You just showing your ass now, girl," she complimented jokingly.

"Always dreamed of having one in a house like this, so I made it happen once I sank my paws into this place," Ta'Jae said before taking a seat behind her desk, motioning for Laney to do the same. "Okay. Now, down to business. I have two questions."

Laney nodded for her to continue after taking a seat on the cute, cushioned chair on the other side of the desk.

"How did you know where to find me, and what was so important that you had to pop up without checking in first?" she asked with serious cautiousness.

"I recognized your house on your Instagram pictures..." Laney was saying before Ta'Jae stopped her mid-sentence with an index finger to the air.

Ta'Jae picked up her phone and made a quick call to Yvonne, telling her to remind her to delete some of her social media photos. "Okay, continue," she encouraged after ending the call.

"Well, I'm here because I just so happen to be stuck in a delicate situation, and I came to see if you would rent me one of your girls."

Ta'Jae sat back in her chair and clasped her hands together while staring hard at Laney, who had caught her off guard with the random and outrageous request. "Those girls are literally like my children and even the worst one brings in at least ten thousand a night. You're going to have to elaborate if I'm even going to consider what you're requesting."

Laney took a deep breath before giving her a general rundown of her undercover war with J-Rock. She didn't share all the details, but she made sure Ta'Jae understood the severity of the situation. "I've worked too hard to get where I am, and I can't just let all of that be snatched away from me. A woman like yourself should understand where I'm coming from... I can't use any of my girls, and I don't have time to raise a toddler, so you're literally my only choice."

Ta'Jae gave her another hard stare before taking a deep breath and sitting up in her chair. "Listen... I'm going to help you only because I see soooo much of my younger self inside of you. You're thriving in this treacherous city, and I also love how you made a way for Mini... It's going to cost you though. Business is business, no matter how much I favor you."

"Just name the price," Laney responded with a bright, brace-faced smile.

She knew she still had a long way to go until J-Rock's demise, but it still felt like a big weight was lifted from her shoulders.

Chapter 8

Meanwhile, on the south side of Charlotte, J-Rock watched as Murk approached with his twelve Vultures in tow. They were a literal kill-squad that handled most of Rock Nation's heavy duty dirty work. They were referred to as The Big Birds by the other members of Rock Nation. If there was a rebellion or a major fuck up somewhere in the chain of command, they'd swoop down like vultures and handle the business in the messiest way possible. Rock Nation had no shortage of killers or enforcers, but Murk and his Vultures put fear in the toughest of the bunch. *Nobody* wanted a visit from them.

Murk handpicked and trained them all to be ruthless, fearless, and psychotic. They only answered to Murk, but J-Rock didn't give a fuck because Murk answered to him. "It's about time, nigga. Glad you can finally make it," J-Rock spat sarcastically.

"Traffic," Murk explained with a nonchalant shrug. "We ready though." Each of them had fully automatic rifles in hand, wearing black from head to toe.

The bridge that they were under shielded them from the heavy rain that descended onto the city. It was a dark, cold night, and they were about to go hunting. Nobody there was nervous or jittery. They were nothing but coldblooded killers ready to get the job done, so they could go on about their lives.

"Y'all go around back and cover shit. Anything that comes out, chop 'em down," J-Rock commanded his five generals. They served as his personal security detail and much more.

They were another group of individuals who were notorious within Rock Nation. Every young soldier dreamed of one day becoming a general. They were like the police of Rock Nation, and the Vultures were the SWAT team. The generals hooded up and jogged off with their guns in hand.

"Y'all bulldoze the front and do what y'all do best," J-Rock said to Murk, who gave the nod to the Vultures.

They watched as the Vultures quickly made their way across the street, toward the secluded warehouse that they were targeting. Murk had them practicing on a real tactical course, with a real ex-SEAL trainer, so their formation was professional.

"They been running their operation so smoothly, without a threat from us for so long, so they feel like they're safe. Well, tonight, I'm pulling up with a promise and not a fucking threat," J-Rock spat grimly before walking off into the rain.

Murk just shook his head, pulled his pistol from his waistband, and followed.

They took their time crossing the street purposely, letting most of the damage play out before they stepped into the warehouse. Once they were inside of the warehouse, the Vultures had most of the Colombians pinned down as they tried to protect their fort. They had received a huge shipment of cocaine and weren't going down without a fight.

"Finish 'em off!" Murk barked enthusiastically from the distance as he and J-Rock took cover.

The next thing they heard was a flash bang, a few more shots, and the all clear from one of the Vultures.

"They getting better at this shit," J-Rock noted as they continued into the warehouse.

They eyed all the bricks of cocaine being prepared for distribution. It was the fucking motherload, and J-Rock couldn't help but rub his hands in prayer position while licking his lips. It would be his biggest come-up in history. Shit was about to turn up a notch.

"The rest of them are holed up in that room. About three or four tops," Swiss informed. He was Murk's top Vulture and righthand man.

J-Rock smiled. "Fernandooooo! If I got to come in there, I'm going to kill everybody in that bitch. Now, I'm just trying to talk. I never took you as the type to be hiding with your tail tucked while bullets flying."

Fernando was the muscle for the Blue Guerillas in Charlotte. They were a branch off of the M-19 Guerillas, who hunted Pablo Escobar back in the day. They were responsible for most of the cocaine that came into Charlotte, and Fernando was the muscle of the organization. He made his mark on the south side of Charlotte in the early 2000s. He wasn't to be fucked with. All the old heads could tell you stories about the crazy Colombian they called Fernando and how he had held the organization together ever since then.

J-Rock had a sweet deal with the Blue Guerillas, and he received his coke at a very generous discount. So, the gangs could sell it for him at an impressive profit. That arrangement worked for J-Rock for a long while, but now that he had the muscle and recourses to take on the Gulf Clan Cartel, who backed the Blue Guerillas, he was making his move.

"Chimba!" Fernando spat as he exited the back room of the warehouse with his three soldiers in tow. It meant *pussy* in Colombian. "I never tuck my tail. You know what I'm made of," he barked defiantly with his head held high.

J-Rock clapped his hands in applause. "I knew I could count on you to do the right thing, nigga." He took off his hoodie and looked around the warehouse. "This is a big shipment you got right here. How often do these come in?"

"I'm not into foreplay. I like to get straight to the fucking," Fernando spat before raising his pistol, trying to take J-Rock out with him in a blaze of glory, but the Vultures cut him down before he could even get a single shot off, along with the rest of his soldiers.

J-Rock took a deep breath, unfazed. "Get all of this dope over to the main stash spot and make sure y'all burn this bitch all the way to the ground. Burn it from the inside out. Put extra gasoline on the bodies," he instructed before continuing out the back where his generals waited on him.

Chapter 9

The next afternoon, Laney woke up earlier than usual. She felt a little better because Ta'Jae had agreed to help her. J-Rock had a thing for the things that he couldn't have, and one look at Ta'Jae's girl would make J-Rock want her because he knew his ugly ass wasn't meant to have her. Once she was in good with J-Rock, Laney would carry on her plan from there.

She had a meeting with Ta'Jae's girl, Vanya, this evening before she was due at the lounge. She missed her man and tried to call him on Messenger's video chat, but it rang out. She called two more times and received the same result. She knew Zion saw her fucking calls because he had just posted a story about twelve minutes ago, and his green light was on, insinuating that he was active.

She didn't trip though. She just shot him an apologetic message instead before heading into Mini's room to check on her. She wasn't inside when Laney had gotten home. She left out of her room and headed down the hall to Mini's little palace of a room. It was purple with stuffed animals every damn where.

She spotted Mini sprawled across her queen-sized bed in a Powerpuff Girls onesie. Laney smiled because the little bitch was still a kid at heart. Most people on the outside looking in probably thought that the childishness was just an act to make herself seem cuter to guys, but Laney knew that it was way deeper than that. Like Laney, Mini never got to have too much of a childhood growing up in the system. It wasn't until Laney started looking after her when she was eleven that Mini knew what if felt like for someone to actually have her back with no strings attached.

They had met seven years ago, back when Laney was still working the pole. She was in the mall, shopping for herself in Macy's, when Mini caught her eye. The little girl was just standing off in the distance, watching her shop. Her hair was nappy, and she was dusty all around the board, looking like nobody loved her, like the girl who would never have a birthday party of her own, but Laney still smiled and waved because she related. Mini smiled back.

Laney went back on with her shopping until she heard a commotion. The store's security had Mini by the arm as Mini struggled to get away, cursing at the man.

She didn't even think before reacting. She just sprang into action, moving one foot in front of the other as she closed the distance between them. "If you don't get your muthafucking greasy hands off my daughter, I know something!" she barked with a voice so defiant that the man let her go instantly. Laney had one hand in her purse and both eyes peering up at him.

"I-I caught her stealing, ma'am," he explained while pointing at Mini, who stood there like a deer in headlights.

Laney shifted her peering eyes to Mini. "Give it back!"

Mini slowly lifted up her jacket and pulled some jeans and a sweater out from underneath. She handed the outfit to the man slowly.

"Now, apologize to this mam for stealing out of his store!" Laney commanded sternly. For someone who never had a mother herself, she had the mother role down pat.

"I'm sorry for stealing the clothes," Mini apologized, just over a whisper.

"I know how it is these days, and I'm sorry for grabbing your daughter," the security guard apologized before going about his business.

When he was gone, Laney gave Mini a look. "What's your name, and how old are you?"

"Melissa, but my friends call me Mini. And I just turned eleven."

"And where is your real mother?" Laney asked curiously because there was no way she should be stealing from a store for something better to wear.

Mini shrugged. "I grew up in the group home not too far from here... I was just trying to get some better clothes for school, so them girls don't talk bad about me."

"Damn." That took Laney for a loop. It was at that moment that she saw so much of herself in Mini. She had to hold back tears. "Come on. Follow me."

She took Laney on a small shopping spree and bought her a prepaid phone, programming her number in there. She promised Mini that she would always look out for her and be by her side. They quickly became inseparable, and Laney ended up legally adopting her a year later. It was history from there.

"Wake up, Sleepy Head," she greeted after climbing into the bed with Mini.

Mini stirred then released a prolonged stretch. "Hey, Mommy," she greeted sweetly before grabbing the closest stuffed animal and pulling it close.

"You had fun last night?" Laney asked while playing in her hair.

"No. Broke up with my boyfriend. Now he big mad."

Laney chuckled. "Fuck him! I knew that wasn't going to last anyway... I do got something that'll cheer you up though."

"Whatttt?" Mini asked before turning around, facing her.

"Yo Gotti was supposed to perform at the lounge tonight, but he had to cancel because of an emergency. Folks was expecting for the lounge to be turned up tonight, so I'll give you free rein over the place if you think you can have it jumping in such short notice."

Mini was fully awake now. Laney had her full attention. "Now you know I'm the princess of the city. I bet you they won't even notice Gotti was supposed to be there! Let me get myself together. I'm about to go live right now."

Laney watched as she popped off of the bed and stormed into the bathroom. She smiled and shook her head. She was so proud of the woman that Mini was growing into. There was no telling how she would've turned out if she would've never taken her in. Little did Mini know, Laney needed her just as much. If it wasn't for the responsibility of being there for Mini, Laney didn't know where she would be. They were blessings for each other.

Chapter 10

Later on that afternoon, Laney met Vanya at a Chipotle by her condo. Ta'Jae made it clear that she was to never show up to her palace again. Laney was under a microscope that Ta'Jae couldn't afford to get seen up under. She liked Laney but couldn't embrace her at the moment. Laney respected Ta'Jae's wishes to the fullest extent. Shit, she probably would've been on the same timing if shit was the other way around.

She spotted Vanya sitting at a table alone, enjoying a grilled chicken meal. "Hey, pretty lady."

"Hi," Vanya greeted with a hand over her mouth since it was still full of food.

"Did Ta'Jae tell you exactly what is going to be expected from you? This isn't an easy task, but there is a big reward involved. Plus, I'll forever be in your debt, and that goes a long way in this life."

Vanya looked up at her and nodded her head. "What do I have to do?"

"Have you ever heard of J-Rock and Rock Nation?"

"Yeahhh. I've heard of Rock Nation but nobody named J-Rock," Vanya answered with distant eyes, showing that she was scanning her memory. "I've heard of Rock Nation on the news a few times. Some type of violent gang or something."

"Not necessarily a gang but yeah. You get the picture... Well, J-Rock is the founder of Rock Nation, and he's going to be your target. The mission is clear and simple. Get close to him and gain his trust."

"I guess I can do that... Back in Russia, when I was younger, I used to belong to a branch of the Russian mob. I grew up being abused by men like that. Probably worse. I'm not as fragile as I look," Vanya informed matter-of-factly.

Laney smiled mischievously. "I knew I had picked right last night! It was something in those pretty eyes. I believe you about the fragile part but still... Out here in America, J-Rock is just about as tough as it gets, so I'm still going to need you to be aware."

"Understood. I won't let you, or Ta'Jae, down," Vanya assured sincerely.

****

After schooling Vanya on some more of J-Rock and Rock Nation's history, Laney headed to Lester's apartment a few miles from her condo. She didn't tell him she was coming, so it was an unexpected visit.

He opened the door in sweatpants and a tank top. "What are you doing here?" he asked while rubbing his eyes.

"I was in the neighborhood," she said while walking past him, into his spot. "You ever holler at your cousin out in Chicago?"

"You told me to put a hold on it, remember?" Lester reminded with his head inside of the fridge.

"Oh, yeahhh. Do you think they'll buy all of it? Four bricks isn't just lightweight now." She helped herself to a seat on the couch.

"Nah, he's not getting it like that, but his father is. If we sell 'em at about twenty-two a brick, he'll jump on 'em."

Laney did the math in her head. A free ninety thousand would definitely help her because it would put a dent in the quarter million she had to pay Ta'Jae for Vanya's services. The Russian bitch was expensive, but she knew J-Rock, and she knew what type of bitches he fantasized about. She paid attention back when she used to date Murk, and they used to hang around J-Rock.

"Alright. Set it up... Start recruiting for some more men on my security detail too. At least two more."

"That's probably the best thing to do at this point. At least until the storm is cleared," Lester agreed as he joined her in the living room with a bowl of cereal.

Laney sighed heavily. "It just been sooo damn much going on lately. A bitch might start smoking weed again."

"Nahhh, you been doing real good without it. That shit be having you too drowsy and lazy. Trust me, this the time for you to be clear minded," Lester advised with concern cleat in his voice.

She sighed again before standing up. "Okay, I'll leave it alone... I'll see you later on. Come pick me up at eleven thirty."

"Hold on. I'll follow you," he offered after popping up off of the couch.

"I'll be fine... I drove myself over here, and I can drive home. Just pick me up tonight," she instructed before finding her own way out.

Chapter 11

Later on that night, Static Lounge had turned into a whole nightclub. Mini outdid herself this time. The whole city came out and showed out for her little pretty ass. The best local artists performed, a few actors made an appearance, and just about every drug dealer and bad bitch in the city showed up. It was turning out to be the event of the season.

Laney played the back field and holed up in her office. Mini was running the place like a warden ran a maximum-security prison. She'd watched Laney run the lounge for so long, she'd naturally acquired the skill over the years. Laney watched proudly through the cameras. She really felt the feeling of a proud mother, and it felt so damn good to her.

She left Mini to it and tried to call Zion once again. She knew he'd been purposely ducking her calls, and it was doing something to her. She hated when he got like this. "Ughhhhh! This nigga gets on my fucking nerves!" she vented aloud.

"Zion?" Lester asked with a raised brow, looking up from the crossword puzzle game he played on his phone.

She nodded her head up and down. "He think I'm on some other shit when I don't communicate with him as much as he would like, but little does the nigga understand, a bitch got all this shit going on. I'm literally out here trying to accomplish the impossible."

"I mean, how is he supposed to know if you won't tell him? Right now, he's on the outside looking in. How can you blame him for not understanding when you never gave him the chance to understand?"

She gave him a blank stare. "And you would take his fucking side!"

"As much as I like Zion, if I had to choose sides between the two of y'all, I'd choose you without a second thought. You know that, but wrong is wrong, and right is right. I'm going to tell you when you're wrong just like I tell you you're right," he stated logically with one leg now crossed over the other, like someone's therapist.

"And I hate when you're right," she admitted reluctantly. "Let me text this man something that'll make him call me back."

"You should start paying me a therapist check as well," Lester joked with a smirk.

Laney just looked up at him through sharp, squinted eyes that could kill.

****

Armondo took down his eighth shot since arriving at the bar. He'd been drinking all day, so he showed up at the bar already drunk. His whole life had been shitted on, and he was grieving heavily.

"Another!" he ordered, looking at the sexy bartender through glossy eyes.

The brunette bartender gave him a concerned look. "I think you've had enough, sir."

"I paid for my fucking membership, and that comes with free drinks. The brochure never said anything about how many. Now pour me another drink!" he commanded forcefully.

The bartender poured him another shot to shut him up but made sure to call her boss and report his behavior.

Ten short minutes later, Ta'Jae strolled into her bar, sexily dressed in a lavender dress and Giovanni heels. She had a full bar in the basement of her palace that stayed open to members of the Midnight Club. When Yvonne called, informing her that Armondo was in the bar causing a disturbance, she paused her paperwork and headed straight down there.

Armondo was one of the first members of the Midnight Club. He was one of the city's most elite businessmen and basically became a good friend and advisor to Ta'Jae over the years. He was a smart, collective, and calm man at all times, so for her to be receiving a complaint about him was insane. He usually gave her advice and kept her on her toes. This was a very foreign situation. She had to go check things out for herself.

"Armondo. How are you doing tonight?" she asked gently after taking a seat at the bar next to him.

He took a deep breath and looked at her with a sadness he couldn't hide. "It's all bad, buttercup," he admitted, calling her the nickname he'd made for her.

"You want to go somewhere else and talk about it? Looks like you've had all you could drink. I'd hate for you to catch alcohol poison," she suggested gently, not trying to offend him in any way.

He took another deep breath and nodded his head up and down. She offered to help him up, but he declined and stood on his own. He was a little wobbly, but he obviously held his liquor well for an old man because he followed her all the way upstairs to one of the sitting rooms. They sat across from each other in two chairs with a crystal chessboard in between them on a crystal table.

"So, talk to me. What's going on because this isn't you at all. I've known you for ten long years, and I've *never* seen you out of character," she noted seriously.

Armondo took another deep breath as he looked at her, slouched in his seat. "I lost my very favorite little cousin and millions of dollars in the same night. It's a lot to handle, buttercup. It's a lot."

"Damn! I can't even imagine something like that happening to me," she admitted. "Is there anything I can do to help? You've helped me in one of my dark times, and I never forget a favor."

Armondo shook his head from side to side. "Not unless you know of any hitmen that aren't scared to take out the leader of Rock Nation," he blurted out but immediately realized his mistake. "Shit! You never heard me say that!"

Ta'Jae looked at him with wide eyes of pure surprise. All these years, she never knew that Armondo got his hands dirty — maybe a few white-collar crimes, taking shortcuts around the IRS maybe, but nothing like this. He carried his image so elegantly and professionally that no one would suspect him of being involved in the streets. He was personal friends with the fucking mayor for fuck's sake.

"I mean, I'm going to disregard what was said regardless... But I think I may know someone who would be a good ally to you. Someone that's already risking their life to bring J-Rock down," she informed matter-of-factly.

Armondo instantly sobered up a little at the mention of J-Rock's name. "Who?"

Chapter 12

"It's been two days, and this bitch ass nigga still ain't reached out yet," J-Rock stated irritably.

"That nigga probably devastated right now. You took a lot from that nigga. He got to bounce back," Tory stated, putting himself in Armondo's shoes. He was Rock Nation's five-star general and J-Rock's closest confidant. He was the only person outside of Static and Murk that could speak to him without a filter.

"You think he going to reach out soon, or we need to pay him a visit?" J-Rock asked.

Tory gave him a knowing look, looking like the rapper Blac Youngsta. "Bruh, you sent the nigga a picture of his main mans laid out, dead as hell. Trust me, he going to reach out soon enough... I don't even know why it should matter though, my nigga. We got the shipment now. That's millions of dollars' worth of dope. We the plug now."

J-Rock tightened his robe up before taking his shot on the pool table in his dining room, where the table should've been. They were at his house, gambling. "See, you not looking at the bigger picture, dawg. Armondo had connections that we need. He's plugged in with the real plug. The muthafuckas in Colombia that actually make the shit. The real deal cartel. I'm trying to get plugged in with them, and he's the middleman."

"I guess that makes sense, but in the meantime, let's focus on getting all these bricks off," Tory encouraged before taking another shot. He missed.

J-Rock stood there and nodded his agreement. "Yeah, you right... Go ahead and set up a meeting with the heads of all the gangs within Rock Nation. We need to have a roundtable."

Tory dropped his pool stick on the table, grabbed his car keys, and headed out. J-Rock moved the balls and took a seat on top of the table. He had so much power in his hands, but he couldn't even enjoy it because he wanted more. He had nearly a thousand soldiers at his command and millions of dollars at his disposal, but he wanted more. His hunger obviously couldn't be tamed.

****

The next morning, Laney called an emergency meeting at her place. Mini had slept over at one of her friend's house, so Laney took the opportunity to handle some business. The meeting was for her puppies. That was what she called the girls that she pimped, and she made them address her as Boss Lady.

"Alright... I know I gave y'all bitches a break for the past two days, and that's unusual. Shit, I've probably been acting unusual, but there's good reason for that, and that's exactly what this meeting is for," she stated clearly.

She sat on top of the kitchen bar counter, dressed in a tight, dark green, Adidas tracksuit, peering down at them seriously. She was responsible for all fifteen of them and took her responsibility very seriously. "I shut operations down at the club because shit is hot right now. Shit, the reason we're not having this meeting at the lounge right now is because shit is hot. I had time to have this place swept for bugs but not the lounge since it's much bigger."

"Bugs? Like the little listening devices? What's going on, Boss Lady?" Yummy asked curiously. She was one of Laney's top bitches, which was why she was speaking in a meeting without permission.

"Yeah, exactly. The lil' listening devices... The Feds are investigating us, and J-Rock himself is investigating us as well. There's a whole war going on underneath the surface, and it's a war I intend to come out on top of. Just let me worry about that though. All I need from you bitches is to do exactly what I say, how I say it, and when I say it. I need your complete loyalty and devotion, now more than ever. Shit's getting real these days."

Missy twisted her face up. "Fuck the Feds and muthafuck J-Rock! We riding with you until the whole car fall apart! You got this, Boss Lady. We all got faith in you fasho. You always find a way through, and this time is nothing different. You got this." She was Laney's first top bitch and most trusted. Laney had bought her from an abusive pimp, which was why Missy felt like she was forever in Laney's debt.

Laney was touched as she watched the rest of the girls nod in agreement to Missy's strong statement. These bitches had just about more faith in her than she had in her own damn self, and that meant everything. Just like Mini, they were also a part of her legacy, so she would protect them at all costs.

"I swear I love y'all bitches," she admitted but with a straight face. She felt deeply for them but never showed too many feelings to them though. She had to remain firm with them. "Listen up though... Like I said, there are going to be some changes made. I'm reconstructing the whole operation now. Give me like two more days and we're going to be back making money as usual. I'm going to pass orders and instructions down to the boss bitches, that'll pass them down to the rest."

She hopped off the counter and pulled her pants all the way onto her ass. "Alright, go on about your business. I'm about to get some sleep... The ones that's scheduled to work the club tonight need to be there early because I'm having a staff meeting later on too... Lock my door behind you, Missy," she instructed before walking off to her room.

Chapter 13

After the meeting with her puppies, Laney laid down and checked her phone. Zion had texted her back, but it wasn't what she had hoped for. He basically told her that he understood where she was coming from and to keep living her life. She couldn't provide details over text, so he probably took her saying she had a lot going on as her dealing with another man.

She didn't have the energy to text him back right then, so she got some sleep. She woke up later on that evening and texted him, confessing her love and devotion to him before pleading for him to return her calls. They both had enormous pride and took turns swallowing it. She figured it was her turn, so she did that.

After sending the text, she got ready and headed out. She was frustrated and needed a release, so she headed around the corner to her plaything's apartment. Platinum was a little secret of hers that she had kept for years. He was a sexy chocolate action figure of a man that made his money stripping at the male strip club not too far from the lounge. Mini, Lester, and Static didn't know about him, but Zion did.

When she met Zion on Facebook two years ago and he admitted how he found it hard to believe that she wasn't getting any dick out there, she let him know about Platinum and the role he played in her life. After they began to get serious about their relationship, she vowed to kick Platinum to the curb, but Zion stopped her from doing so.

He reminded her that he was the one incarcerated, and not her, so he didn't want her depriving herself on account of him. He suggested that she keep Platinum around for when she needed to get her rocks off. He only had one condition, and that was to keep her heart out of the situation, which was easy for her. They agreed on the arrangement and *never* spoke on it again.

She showed up at Platinum's doorstep, and his black, sexy self was right there waiting on her. "It's been a lil' minute. Miss Big Daddy, huh?" he asked with a sly smirk.

"Shut up, nigga, and take them shorts off," she commanded as she pushed him backward into the apartment and closed the door behind them.

"Shit, you ain't even have to tell me once. I can't wait to get up in them guts," he admitted while following orders.

Laney didn't have too much undressing to do after taking off her peacoat. All she had to wat slip out of the mini skirt she wore underneath, and she was fully naked. "Ohhh, shit, you know I like when you pick a bitch up like that."

He had her up in the air, up over his head, using the living room wall for support. She put one leg over the back of his shoulder and both hands on the top of his head for support as he covered her clit with his mouth. He sucked on it like a baby bottle and started rocking his head slightly.

"Yesssss, muthafuckaaaa! Good God! Don't you dare stop!" she ranted intensely with both eyeballs watching the back of her head.

Platinum did as he was told and continued eating her pussy like his favorite meal. After she came, he let her down, but she was still in his arms. He carried her over to the couch, where he sat her down on top of his dick after putting on a condom.

"I'm not going to force it. Ride that dick at your own pace. Do your thing," he challenged smoothly.

She rolled her eyes. "Fuck all that Casanova shit. I keep telling you we not making love, nigga... Beat this pussy up!"

"Say less!" he agreed before wrapping his hands around her small waist and pounding away at her guts.

"Yup-yup-yuppp! That's it, nigga! Keep it comin!" she encouraged as her juicy ass cheeks clapped together on his dick.

He picked her back up without warning. She was about to complain because she didn't like getting fucked in the air for some reason, but before she could say anything, he sat her back down on the couch, facing the opposite direction. Back shots was exactly what she needed. They hit the spot every time.

"Show no mercy," she challenged as she put an impressive arch in her back.

Platinum clenched his teeth and rammed himself inside of her. "Just when I thought that pussy couldn't get any wetter." She was creaming up something serious.

Like always, he rose up to the challenge and dicked her down properly. "Oweee! Faster, niggggggaaaa!"

He wrapped both hands around her neck and applied pressure before putting one leg up on the couch and plowing away at her little pussy. Before he knew it, she was shaking uncontrollably and pushing him off of her.

"Woahhh! What the hell you doing?" he asked with a crumbled face as he watched her stumble over to where her skirt laid on the floor.

"What it look like, nigga?" she asked, heavy on the sarcasm.

He literally stood there with his dick in his hand. "This your second time pulling this stunt. You really going to do a nigga like this?"

"Your purpose is to get me off. Once I get my rocks off, I'm gone... You got to figure out the rest yourself, my boy," she retorted after pulling her skirt up.

"I'm really getting tired of you treating me like a lame or something. Like what kind of shit is that?" He complained seriously. "You got a nigga bent for real."

"Nobody's forcing you to fuck with me, bookie. If you feel like that, lose my number," she countered nonchalantly before finding her own way out of his spot.

Chapter 14

Laney was on her way back to her spot, so she could shower and spend some time with Mini before it was time for work. The rainy streak still hadn't ended, and a light ran had begun to fall onto the city for the fourth straight day. She was at a red light, waiting on the green, when a limousine drove up and stopped directly in front of her truck, blocking her off.

A professionally dressed, Hispanic man hopped out and quickly made his way to the driver's window, motioning for her to roll it down. Her heart accelerated, and her fear began to rise as she quickly put her truck in reverse, but there was nowhere for her to go. Another car had already pulled behind her bumper to bumper. They had to be working together.

The Hispanic man tapped on her window again, but this time, it was with a pistol. "We just want to talk! Don't turn this into something it's not supposed to be! Put the car in park and get out!" he shouted in perfect English.

She took a deep breath, trying to control her fear. She'd never been ambushed before, and it wasn't fun. Her mind was racing a million different ways, trying to figure out what they wanted with her. Her best guess was that it had to be an agent with the Feds coming to offer her a deal to snitch. Either way, it didn't look like she had a choice, so she was sure to find out very soon.

She put the truck in park, grabbed her purse, and got out of the truck. Another well-dressed Hispanic man got out of the car behind her and got in the driver's seat of her truck. "He's going to follow us in it," the first man informed as he escorted her to the limousine.

She climbed into the back of the limousine, wiped the water off of her face, and looked up at a well-dressed Hispanic man, but this one was way older and had a lot more class about himself. He was obviously the boss of the motorcade and the reason for her presence.

The driver pulled off immediately after they were inside.

"You can relax. No one's going to do anything to you. If I wanted you to be dead, I would've had it done in your sleep earlier today at your condo," he assured in perfect English as well. His grey, silky hair was slicked back, and he had his dress shirt unbuttoned, showing his grey chest hair. Even at his old age, he was still an attractive man.

"What do you want from me?" she asked curiously. This man was nobody's officer. Just one of his diamond rings alone probably cost just as much as her Maserati. He was a boss of some sort.

She clutched onto her purse tightly, waiting for the right moment to dig inside of it, so she could brandish her pearl .380 that she kept with her. She had a daughter to make it home to, and she planned on doing so.

"Calm down. You don't have to be so tense," he assured smoothly before taking a puff from a smelly cigar. His eyes were steady on hers, and it seemed like he didn't blink. They just stayed open. "I actually come as a friend and not an enemy."

"And who are you exactly?" she asked impatiently. The suspense was killing her.

"My name is Armondo," he greeted gently. "I am a very successful businessman and own about one fourth of the houses and apartment buildings on the south side of the city. I also own a handful of restaurants and laundromats there as well."

"That still doesn't tell me what the hell you want with me though." She pointed out, ready to cut to the chase.

"Impatient woman, I see," he noted aloud. "I guess you have good reason for that under the circumstances... You're here because we have a mutual enemy. I wasn't always a successful businessman. I used to be the leader of the Blue Guerillas back in the day before I handed the reins over to my cousin, Fernando, about ten years ago. Everything was smooth up until a few days ago when J-Rock took millions of dollars in coke from me, along with my cousin's life."

Laney sat there with wide eyes, piecing everything together. If he was telling the truth, then she had herself an ally, but something was missing. "And what makes you think that J-Rock is an enemy of mines?"

"Because our mutual friend is Ta'Jae."

****

J-Rock and Murk took their weekly trip to the luxury rental car dealership to switch their whips out. It was a safety precaution that J-Rock had been practicing for years, and now that Murk was royalty in Rock Nation, he had to do the same. The president and the vice president had to be protected *at all costs*, which was why they were usually followed by small motorcades.

They parked their old cars out front, with the keys inside, and headed into the oversized building. The CEO approached them like clockwork, looking like a well-dressed young version of Johnny Depp. "My favorite guy!" He was referring to J-Rock.

"Waddup, D?" J-Rock returned the greeting with a smirk. D was short for Devin.

"Step over here with me," D suggested while motioning toward a Lamborghini truck that was spinning slowly on a platform. "Let me show you my newest piece."

J-Rock followed Devin, and Murk went his own way, trying to see what whip he wanted to push that week.

"I have these in all basic colors," Devin informed. "I thought about you when they arrived."

"Oh, you know I got to pop it off with a black one... But fuck that truck. What's the business?" J-Rock asked in a serious tone.

"I was at a fundraiser the other night, rubbing elbows with the police commissioner, and I'm not going to lie. It's not looking good at all. I suggest you lawyer up immediately and brace yourself. They're closing in on you, my friend."

J-Rock had been renting cars from Devin for a whole year before he sank his paws into him. Like every other rich, white kid, he was in need of the ultimate thrill and rubbing elbows with the leader of the most ruthless organization that Charlotte had ever seen got his rocks off pretty well. J-Rock didn't even have to pay him for the information he provided. He just wanted to be down, so according to J-Rock, he was the only Caucasian in Rock Nation.

"What the fuck you mean? What exactly did he say? I need some details because they been on my ass for over fifteen years, and I'm still here. They going to have to use more than some scare tactics when it come to me."

Devin took a deep breath before adjusting his three-piece suit. "We already knew about the investigation, which is why I decided to spark a conversation with him in the first place. I started talking about car thefts that I've been having problems with, then we eventually started talking about the overall crime rate in the city, so you know Rock Nation came up. He said something about some brave witnesses that would finally be your downfall and how he couldn't wait to make a trophy with the head of the snake."

"What the fuck? Witnesses?" J-Rock's face was twisted up bad as his mind raced, wondering who the witnesses could be.

Devin nodded. "Yes. I tried to get more info out of him, but he figured he had already said too much, and I didn't want to make him suspicious by pressing too hard."

"It's all good, D. You did a good job, and I'll take it from here... Go get that Lamborghini ready for me though."

Chapter 15

Laney made it back to her spot and hopped straight into the shower. Thoughts of Armondo filled her mind. An ally was exactly what she needed at the moment because it was no secret that she was in over her head, going up against J-Rock. She knew all about the Blue Guerillas and how they supplied the city with coke for decades. That equaled a lot of money, and that type of money came with power and connections.

Armondo struck her as a smart man, who was obviously used to power. She knew he was smart because the first move he made against J-Rock was recruiting her. That took restraint and brains, the type of qualities Laney admired in a man. She rode around in the back of the limo, chopping it up with Armondo, as they picked each other's brains and felt each other out. By the time the ride was over with, they were both satisfied with each other and felt more confident about taking J-Rock down.

She got out of the shower, got dressed for the night, and headed into Mini's room to check on her. "Where's my little princess?" she asked as she walked into Mini's room.

"I'm in here!" Mini shouted from her walk-in closet.

Her closet wasn't as big as Laney's, but it was still three times larger than your average walk-in. She had it set up like a small designer store, just like Laney's. They were big on fashion, and there weren't too many bitches in the city that could do it like them.

"I have a surprise for you," Mini informed brightly while scanning a wall of shoes with a hand on her hip. "I've been waiting on you to get home, so I could tell you in person."

"Bitch, you better not be pregnant!" Laney spat, quickly closing the distance between them.

Mini rolled her eyes and flipped her hair back. "Uhmmmm, no! I'm still a baby my damn self. You don't have to worry about becoming a grandma for at least another ten years."

"Okay," Laney said with much relief. "What is it then?"

"Okay. You're about to be really proud of a bitch too."

"Come on, tell me, girl! You got me all worked up now. What is it? What you done got into now, little girl?" Laney asked curiously, but she was clearly excited.

Mini turned toward her with a wide smile. "I've just been selected to star in a Netflix reality showwwww!" she stated but ended up screaming.

Laney stood there, openmouthed. "I know you fucking lying, girl! For reallll though?"

"Yasssss, bitch!" Mini answered with a flick of her wrist. "It's called *IG Baddies*. This wealthy Instagram model is making it. She said she wants to give young, Black women exposure as a form of giving back to her people. I've been following her for a while after she married this billionaire a few months ago, and she never followed me back, so I was surprised when she hopped in my DM earlier today with the offer. It's strictly promotional to get our names out there and gain us fame, so there's no big paycheck though."

"Damn, Mini... I don't even know what the fuck to say. I'm literally beyond proud of you. I always knew you would go on to do even greater things than me," Laney said before pulling Mini in for a big hug.

Mini hugged her back for a brief moment then wiggled out her grasp. "Thank you, Mommy. That's not all though... We're going to be filming the show in a mega mansion out in LA, and it's going to take six months. I have to leave next week... All expenses will be paid though."

Laney was openmouthed again. A Netflix series was no small thing. Mini had just stumbled into a huge opportunity. At first, Laney started to become sad at the thought of going without Mini for that long, but then, she remembered her current circumstances and realized that this was God. She would be able to fully focus with Mini out of harm's way. So, in her mind, she had six months to complete her mission.

"On one condition," she bargained, locking eyes with Mini.

"What?" Mini asked with a raised brow as she brushed her hair in the mirror.

"You let me hire you a personal bodyguard."

Mini rolled her neck. "Oh, no, hunny. I do not need a Lester breathing down my neck. I still don't know how you do it."

"Calm down. He won't be anything like Lester. I'm going to make sure he's as close to your age as possible, tall, light, and easy on the eyes, just how you like 'em. It'll make me feel better about you being on the other side of the country alone."

Mini shrugged her bare shoulders. "I guess... It might be a good look for me on the show. I'll probably be the only bitch on there with my own security with my fake bougie ass. Just make sure he's very, very easy on the eyes."

"Yes, ma'am," Laney responded with a smile.

Her little baby was growing so damn fast, and she was making her mother proud. Laney had raised her right, and the results were showing. The sky was obviously the limit with her little princess.

****

J-Rock was perceived as the most fearless of them all, but that couldn't be the furthest thing from the truth. If he was as fearless as the legends made him out to be, then he wouldn't be so damn paranoid. He would've been dead by now. Everyone had their fears, and J-Rock was no different. He feared not being feared, so he always did what it took to forever remain feared. It gave him satisfaction knowing that even the government feared him enough to focus on him so much, which was crazy. He knew that. He accepted his craziness, but he had never been stupid, and he knew something had to be done about it.

He lounged comfortably on a leather couch in the display room of his favorite upscale furniture store. He went there a few times out of the week to get his thoughts straight. He knew it was weird because he actually had the same exact couch at his place, but it wasn't the couch that did it for him. It was the aura that he received from the store. It was a peaceful place for him. His soul could charge there.

He even had his wheat Timberlands parked on the coffee table. He had an understanding with the owner, so the employees didn't bother him. They just let him do his thing.

"Uhmmm... I'm looking at the way you're lounged on that couch, and I'm wondering if I should go ahead and buy this set. You look truly comfortable," said a stunning mixed woman, who dressed businesslike. It looked like she was fresh out of a corporate meeting.

J-Rock followed the voice with his eyes and laid his eyes on a whole prize stallion. "As comfortable as a muthafucka can get... I'll buy the set for you if you let me take you out to dinner, so you can thank me for drawing you to the best set in the whole store."

She laughed briefly. "That seems like a fair exchange to me. I'm busy today, but I'm off tomorrow evening."

"Aight, say less." He hopped onto his feet and closed the distance between them with his phone out. "Go ahead and put your number in there."

She grabbed his phone and saved her contact before handing it back. "There."

"Vanya, huh? Where's that from?"

"Russia," she answered while looking up at him with those big, pretty eyes.

Chapter 16

"Oh, now you make time for me," Laney spat after answering the phone for Zion. He finally decided to break his silence. "I swear you got me fucked up, nigga."

He was her best friend, and she needed him now more than ever at this moment of her life.

"I missed you too, sexy mama... What'd I miss?" he asked coolly.

She started to give him the bullshit short version of an answer but stopped herself mid-thought. Lester was right. Maybe it was time for her to let him in on her dilemma. "I'm coming to visit you this weekend. We can talk about everything then."

"It's about time your ass came back to Daddy anyway," he agreed. The joy was clear in his voice.

Laney rolled her eyes. He was a real asshole, but she loved him *sooo* much. He was perfect for her in more ways than one. "What's new on your end?"

He told her about his latest problems, but she knew he didn't tell her everything. "I'll be glad when they free your light bright ass. Shit will be so much more simple if you were out here with me."

"I'm on the way sooner than you think," he informed matter-of-factly.

"Speak that shit upppp then, nigga!" she cheered brightly. "Okay, I got to go, baby. I'll talk to you a lil' later on if you're up."

"I'll be up. Just call me, bae," he assured before ending the call.

She felt better after the call. He brought her spiritual joy, and she hoped she really did the same thing for him.

****

Armondo was one of those rare men that you could actually count on in this day and age, a stand-up guy who would literally *never* cross his own, which was why he had been favored by the cartel for decades. Every single one of the narcos he started with back in Colombia were either dead or in prison. That said a lot about him, and he was highly respected for it.

That was why when he made the call informing that he'd lost the last shipment and he needed reinforcements, the cartel sent their best without question. After all, Armondo had never had any complications or asked for any favors up until now.

"You're late," Karmen noted as she painted her toenails on the bed. She was one of the best handlers for the Port Clan Cartel. It was the top cartel in all of Colombia.

Armondo was summoned to Karmen's AirBnB in the downtown area. She figured she'd get comfortable since her stay would be longer than her usual two days. Armondo requesting reinforcements was a state of emergency, so she was pulled out of Dallas and sent straight to him.

"I know. My meeting ran late, and I had to close that deal... Much love for showing up so fast," Armondo greeted as he entered the room with his signature confident stride.

She gave him a knowing look. "The bosses didn't give me a choice... Mind telling me what's this all about? Lay it all out for me. You know I work better when I have all the details."

"I told you five years ago that J-Rock was going to be a problem, and I should have killed him then," he admitted sadly, making a long story short.

Karmen shook her head. "I'm just as much to blame as you. I should've advised you to do it back then... Anyway, what exactly did he do?"

He took a seat on the edge of the bed and turned to face her with one leg on the bed. He told her all about the ambush at the warehouse, Fernando's execution, the stolen coke, and the video that J-Rock sent.

"Show me the video now. I need to feel this," she commanded urgently.

Armondo reluctantly pulled his phone out of his pocket and pulled the email up with the video on there. J-Rock was wearing a body cam, so you never saw him, just what was happening. It started as he walked into the warehouse, and it ended after ordering the warehouse to be burned to the ground.

"Wow." She exhaled. "That was a bit much. Send it to me... Has he contacted you in any way since then?"

He shook his head. "Nope. I'm guessing he's expecting me to make my next move. How many men are on the way?"

"Three six-man teams," she informed as she continued to paint her toenails with the gold polish.

"I don't know how good that's going to do us. That man has an entire army at his disposal, and this city is the base... He's smart. He built up his muscle; now he's exercising."

She nodded her understanding. "I'm aware of that, and that's why we're going to use our brains because we obviously can't win with muscle."

"Speaking of brains, I have someone I want you to meet." He remembered with a smirk.

"If she's not going to be your fourth wife, I don't want to meet her," Karman joked seriously.

He chuckled. "This isn't my lover, but she is an ally... You'll love her. She's a smart young lady."

Chapter 17

The next evening, J-Rock was early to pick up Vanya. She stayed in a decent apartment complex in a good neighborhood on the north side. Tory lounged in the driver's seat while J-Rock was waiting in the backseat of the Lamborghini truck, watching *John Wick* on one of the TV monitors on the back of the front seat. He had just eaten some molly and was feeling himself on a major level.

Ten minutes later, Vanya climbed into the back of the truck with him. "Niceeee." She rocked a long, black, tight fitting, cotton dress.

"This muthafucka like a lil' hotel on wheels. I don't tolerate nothing but the best, which is why you're sitting there now," he complimented in a cocky way. It was obviously the best she was going to get out of him in a sweet sense.

"Well, cheers to that. What are we drinking on this evening?" she asked, signaling she wanted to have fun that night.

"We can order a bottle of wine or champagne when we get to the restaurant," he informed. "I have some molly right now though. You know what that is?"

"Of course I know what molly is," she spat back with a roll of her eyes. "I might seem like a stuck up square, but I promise you this isn't that. Now, let me get a hit of those VVs," she instructed, referring to the current street name for molly.

J-Rock smiled brightly but evilly. "I just *knew* it was something I liked about your ass!" he admitted before pulling out his sack.

They did drugs together and started building a bond together immediately after that. They chopped it up the entire ride to the restaurant, on their way inside, and at the table. J-Rock was impressed by Vanya's versatility. Most bitches that looked like her were snobbish, but she was very down to Earth, just how J-Rock liked them.

"I ain't think you was going to be this cool," he admitted. "I just knew I was going to end up having to cuss you out at some point tonight."

She laughed at his bluntness. "That's funny but thank you for the compliment. I could never forget where I started, so I refuse to be uppity... You're actually cooler than I thought you to be. You're not described as a cool type of person."

J-Rock's paranoia kicked in. "Oh, yeah? And who all described me to you? You did say you heard about me, right?" he asked with a raised brow.

"Calm down, mister... My ex-boyfriend is K-Drop," she answered.

K-Drop was the big homie over Busy Body Gang, the largest gang under Rock Nation. He was killed five years back during a war within the gang. His killer, Big Body, was now the big homie over BBG.

"Damn, he had to have you locked away somewhere because I definitely would've remembered your fine ass."

She nodded with a smile. "Yes, he did. Something about protecting me from his enemies. I just wish I could've protected him from them."

J-Rock stared her down from across the table. He wanted so badly to be suspicious with the bitch, but everything was right about her. An alley boy like him only dreamed about bitches like this, but the two types usually didn't mix. That he knew from experience. Vanya was a different story, a story she made him want to read.

71

"So, what you do for a living? Some type of accountant or somethin'?" he asked curiously, remembering her business attire from the day before.

She shook her head *no*. "I'm an upscale therapist. Rich, white men mostly."

J-Rock nodded his approval slowly. "I can dig that... You found your way out them trenches, and I respect that."

"And so have you, my love," she retorted while returning his intense eye contact.

****

Meanwhile, at Laney's condo, she was spending quality time with Mini before she left. They were baking sugar cookies. She only had a few short days until she was gone. It was weird because they'd never been separated longer than forty-eight hours since they connected. They were going to miss each other very much, but this was for the better.

"I think I found the perfect bodyguard for you. He's young, handsome, and willing to sign a one-year contract to be by your side 24/7. All you got to do is say yes," Laney informed while handing Mini her phone that showed a picture of the bodyguard.

Mini snatched the phone from her and squinted her eyes at the picture. "He's cute or whatever. I guess," she answered before handing the phone back.

"What's wrong?" Laney asked, noticing the change in her energy.

Mini took a deep breath and dropped the cookie cutter. "That shit is going to be hard to enjoy without you. I'm trying to imagine me making it without you, and I just can't see it," she admitted sadly.

"Awww, my baby!" Laney pouted as Mini made her way into her awaiting arms. "You going to do just fine. I raised a smart and beautiful woman. You're rich and about to be famous. Won't nobody be able to run game on you because you learned the game from the best. You'll be well respected and well protected. I'd say you got a better chance of making it than any other girl on that show. Go out there and spread your wings *wide,* baby. I like that you're humble though. That's one of my favorite qualities about you, but don't you dim your shine for *nobody.* You going to be just fine, baby."

"I swear you the best mother in the world. I don't care what nobody say. You the realest bitch alive." Mini squeezed her tighter with watery eyes.

Tears started to actually fall down Laney's eyes though. She couldn't hold it in. "Thank you, baby... We going to talk every single day, and you know Mama going to come visit a few times."

"Now, that will make me feel a lot better."

"Everything going to fall in place, baby. You destined for greatness, no matter what, so you need to hold that head up high. Most of those girls are going to need that show, but you're not. You win regardless of the outcome, so you need to approach it with that attitude. LA will swallow you up if you're soft, so I don't want you taking the soft approach."

Mini rolled her eyes and looked up at her with a hardened stare. Laney was getting in drill sergeant mode. "Come on, Ma. I'm only soft with you and my little boyfriends. You know you raised a baby demon. Those folks ain't fucking with me... I just like being in your nest, but I guess it's time for me to spread my wings."

Laney released her from her grasp, and they went back to making cookies, regrouping from the emotional skit.

Chapter 18

Three days later, it was Zion's visitation day, and Laney was all for it. She got to see and feel the love of her life. He walked into the visitation room looking like a tall god in her eyes.

She stood up and poked out her bottom lip as she extended her tiny arms up at him. He bent down to wrap his hands around her and picked her up in the air, so they were face-to-face. Then, they shared a long, slow, passionate kiss.

"Alright now, Mr. Hilltop. That's enough now," the female guard warned from her post by the door.

Zion sat her down, and they took their seats at the small wooden table that separated them. "Girl, you look finer and finer every time you bring your lil' ass up here."

"Vice versa, nigga." She returned the compliment. "I can't wait until your ass is up out of here."

"It's coming sooner than soon. I'm telling you. They fucked up on my case, bae," he assured faithfully. "I can't give you no exact date though, but I feel like it's going to be soon."

"As long as you got faith, I do as well, bae," she assured. "You want some food?"

"Now, you know I want them hot wings. Buy me three plates this time. I ain't ate shit all day," he instructed while rubbing his slight pudge. "Plus you know I want to see that ass jiggle when you walk away."

She blushed hard. "You so damn aggravating. Hold on, boy."

She went to fulfil his order, and he patiently watched her from his seat.

"They ain't have no more Sprite, so I got you two orange juices instead," she informed while placing his stuff on the table.

"'Preciate that, bae. You always know what a nigga want... All you got is Skittles for yourself? After all this time and all these visits, you still too shy to eat in front of me. That's crazy," he noted amusingly.

"Leave me alone... I just like watching you eat."

He nodded his understanding. "Okay, well, you can talk while I eat. You did have shit you needed to tell me, right?" he asked with a raised brow.

She took a deep breath and struggled on an opener. She didn't know where to start. "Okay... I know I been kind of distant and withdrawn lately, but shit done got real on my end, bae. It ain't what you think at all. I'm in the deep end, and I'm trying to keep this ship afloat because I really don't want to drown."

"I thought you was done with the streets, bae. I thought you put all that shit behind you," he stated with a raised brow and a mouthful of chicken.

She gave him a knowing look. "Nigga, I did... I just had to start playing a little dirty lately because there's a lot on the line, and my enemies play filthy."

"Enemies?" He gave her a stern look of disapproval. "What the hell you doin' out there to be having enemies? Tell me exactly what's happening and with who!" he commanded with the firmness of a father.

"Long story short, there's an active investigation on Rock Nation, and since I'm a known affiliate of Murk and J-Rock, they got me tied up into this shit. Me, my business, and my legacy is on the line, so I'm doing what I have to do to stop that from happening, but in order to do that, I have to remove J-Rock from the equation."

Zion sat there, giving her a blank stare. "Oh, so you America's Next Top Assassin now, huh? You trying to take down warlords and shit now? What the fuckkkk, bae?! You listening to yourself right now?"

"Baby, please don't start. I'm not here to argue about what's happening. I'm here to enlighten you on what's happening... I didn't ask for this shit, but those are the cards I was dealt. He probably knows about the investigation by now, but he don't know about my agenda, so I have the upper hand. I just have to make strategic swings at his head."

Zion shook his head with a chuckle. She was definitely the most interesting woman he'd ever been with. In light of her current situation, he wanted to make it home that much more. He knew he could lighten her load if he was out. It crushed him that he wasn't any actual help to his woman when she was in need. "Damn, bae. I got to hurry up and get out this muthafucka."

"Oh, don't worry about it. I got it covered," she assured confidently. "I got allies, and I got a lil spy close to J-Rock."

Zion sighed while shaking his head in disagreement. "Damn, my future wife is a whole ass mob boss," he stated jokingly, trying to lighten the mood.

"I wouldn't say all that now, but I am a boss bitch. And as soon as my boss nigga makes it home to me, we can be bosses together. I don't think the world is ready for that just yet."

"Well, they better get ready because it's coming," he assured comfortingly and seriously as he took her hand into his.

Chapter 19

When Laney got back into her truck, she checked her phone and saw an unread message from Armondo. He instructed her to be at an address later on that night. He didn't say what for, just scheduled a meet with urgency. She'd been expecting to hear from him anyway. She knew he wanted to discuss strategy, and she was looking forward to it.

Later on that night, Lester picked her up, and they headed to the meeting destination. They arrived at a building that rented exotic condominiums not too far from Laney's building. As much money as Laney was touching at the time, the place was still too expensive for her. That was the only reason she was not staying there herself.

They parked out front and made their way into the lobby. Laney wanted to be extra today, so she threw on a black pantsuit under her black, mink jacket. Her red bottom heels and matching shades had her stepping like a boss. Lester followed close behind her, grilling the Colombian bodyguard that awaited them beyond the entrance of the lobby.

"Follow me please," he instructed before leading the way toward the elevators.

They all went up to the eleventh floor and all the way down the hall, where they entered one of the exclusive units. It was spacious and well designed, like in the movies.

"There she is," Armondo said to an attractive, middle aged Colombian woman. They sat on each end of a wraparound couch.

"Come, sit with us. My name is Karmen," Karmen invited and greeted while motioning for Laney to sit in the middle section on the couch, so they'd all be able to talk comfortably.

Laney took a seat and crossed her legs. "No disrespect, but who exactly are you? Armondo didn't tell me anything about you."

"Yeah, that's kind of his thing," Karmen informed with a slow roll of her eyes. "Like I said, I'm Karmen. His handler. His problems are mines and so are his allies. Nice to meet you." She extended her hand.

Laney shook her hand. "Nice to meet you as well... So, do y'all have any plans?"

"We're still placing our pieces on the chessboard at the moment, but I hear you have some plans of your own already. Tell me about that."

Laney told them about her leak in the investigation and Vanya's mission. "I didn't have time to vet her personally, but I feel like she's the perfect girl for the job. I know what type of bitches J-Rock like for real."

"Okay. You know him personally, and you can provide insight that me and Armondo can't... With that being said, what exactly do you think he's trying to accomplish here?" Karmen asked curiously.

Laney stared her hard in the eyes. "Complete underworld dominance in the region. He's fucking insane. But he's not reckless with it. He's a smart psychopath with the heart of a polar bear, and his mentality is spreading through Rock Nation. Every wannabe gangster out here wants to be like J-Rock, and he loves it... Moral of the story, he's power struck. He wants more power."

"So, we'll give it to him," Karmen suggested with a satisfied tone like she had just come up with one of her best ideas.

"What?" Both Armondo and Laney said together, not sure if they had heard Karmen clearly.

"Calm down. We'll be doing ourselves a favor. I'll pour so much weight into his lap that he'll be so busy counting money that he won't be able to see what we're cooking up for his ass," Karmen reasoned.

"So, you're pushing me out and going to hand my whole empire over to those people. That's crazy, Karmen," Armondo stated in disappointment.

Karmen sighed and faced Armondo. "I've always given it to you straight, and I'm not going to stop now, honey. You're one of the lucky ones. The last boss of your time. Just accept your retirement because most bosses don't make it out. Your empire is in the business world now, and we'll continue to support you in a legal way, but cocaine was Fernando's empire. Hate it or not, Fernando's not with us anymore, and you don't have a grip on the streets like he did. As a businesswoman, going in business with Rock Nation is a no-brainer at this point."

Armondo didn't respond.

"Why would you get in bed with J-Rock knowing about the investigation?" Laney asked curiously. Karmen had struck her as a smarter woman than that.

Karmen smiled. Laney was kind of adorable to her. "No, I'm getting in bed with Rock Nation. Someone will step up once J-Rock has fallen... And let me tell you a little something about investigations. They're placed to root out the menaces to society, so if you show them that you don't pose a threat to them and don't do anything stupid, you'll always come out on top. Shit, I've been getting investigated internationally since I was eighteen. I'm thirty-eight now, baby, and never stepped foot inside of a jail cell."

Armondo nodded his agreement.

"So, what's the plan after you become his new plug?" Laney asked curiously. She was intrigued by Karmen. She loved to see powerful women. It made her proud.

"I'm going to leave that up to you to decide. I'm looking forward to seeing how you're going to handle this situation. You have more invested, and you're more at risk than either of us, so you should run point on this. We'll give you all the assistance you need, but you're going to have to get on the chalkboard and put in the work."

Laney was too far down the road to turn back now. She had to see it through. This was her history to write, and she knew what she had to do, but she still hadn't figured exactly how she was going to do it. "I'll get it done."

"Here. I want you to have this. It fits you, plus it's one of my good luck charms," Karmen said after tossing Laney a diamond tennis chain with a ruby rose pendant.

Laney picked the chain up and examined the beautiful piece. "Why you giving me this?"

"It's just my way of saying good luck, baby. Don't think too much on it. Material things mean nothing to me anymore."

Laney should've said more but just nodded her thanks.

"Ooookayyy... We covered some ground and even have a plan in motion on the very first meeting. We make a good team and all, but I'm going to have to take me a shower. I have a date scheduled in approximately thirty minutes, which I'm going to be late for, so I'm going to excuse myself. Make yourselves at home if you're not ready to leave yet. My cook is on the way as we speak," Kristen informed before getting up and disappearing around a corner.

"You're a special woman. She doesn't speak to most people with respect... You'll see," Armondo stated seriously.

"What's her story though?" Laney asked curiously.

Armondo shook his head side to side. "That's a long story there. Just listen when I tell you she's *not* a friendly person, so for her to give you a gift means a lot. She took a leap of faith in you, so just never cross her. She will have you killed."

Laney swallowed the lump in her throat and nodded her understanding. She was all in now, so she just had to make sure she continued to play it smart. She dreamed of making it as long as Karmen had in the game.

Chapter 20

After the meeting, Laney made her way to meet Vanya. This time, they met in a dark downtown alley. They couldn't afford being seen in public again.

Lester pulled up alongside Vanya's Toyota Camry as he rolled the back window down for Laney. "I see you survived date number one. I'm impressed."

"Just like you predicted, he's eating out of the palm of my hand. He's actually cooler than you let on. We have more in common than I could've ever guessed."

Laney gave her a satisfied look. "That's what I'm talking about, girl. I knew you was the one... Might have to give you a bonus if you get close enough fast enough."

"By the looks of things, he'll be trying to marry a bitch in a few months," Vanya confidently predicted.

Laney nodded her approval with a pretty smile. "Whatever you're doing, keep it up... Just go on about your life as usual, and I'll be in touch soon. You get in touch with me if it's something important you think I should know."

Lester pulled off down the alley as Laney rolled her own window up. She sat back and sighed, but this time, it was a sigh of relief. Her ducks were lined up, and she had some foundation. Now, it was time to build.

She picked one of her phones up off of the seat and texted Zion, letting him know how much he was missed. If only he knew what she had in store for him upon his return to society.

He was a breadwinner his damn self, even in prison, but she was ready to spoil his ass with love and material.

"You want to reschedule this last meeting for tomorrow since it's so late? I know you want to check up on the club before after hours," Lester said while glancing at her in the rearview mirror.

Laney shook her head. "Let's get it out of the way tonight. All my spare time is going to Mini tomorrow."

"I got a serious question for you... I usually let you just make your own decisions and advise when I see fit, but we're obviously heading into deeper waters. So, as the head of your security, I need to be kept in the loop, so I can protect you properly."

"I can do that... What's the question though, bruh?"

"What's your big plan for J-Rock? You only have two options. Get him locked up or get him killed. Both have their consequences," he noted at the end.

"There won't be any consequences when it comes to killing him because I'm going to have my shit sealed up tight," she assured seriously.

"I'm not saying you're not, but there are other possible consequences though," he warned. "What if Murk doesn't have what it takes to get the generals in line? Rock Nation will be divided and so will all the gangs up under Rock Nation. That will bring back street wars and all type of other shit that'll end up being a headache for you sooner or later."

"J-Rock will be a headache sooner or later, even if he goes to prison for the rest of his life... He has to go, bruh. It's something that has to be done."

Lester nodded his understanding with his eyes on the road. "I'm with you one hundred percent, and these guys I just recruited will be as well."

"I'm definitely ready to see who you picked," she admitted before reading a text that Zion had just sent.

"They're ready to see you too," Lester retorted with a chuckle.

****

Lester pulled up to a big bar in the west side area. It used to be one of his favorite places to drown his sorrows in. Now, he owned the place. He bought it with money that he'd been able to hustle up doing side gigs for Laney, and he bought it because it was like a reminder of where he came from. This would be the first time he'd stepped foot in there for three years though. Nobody there even knew he was the owner. He did business with the manager through email.

Laney walked inside first with Lester hot on her heels. Thankfully, the place wasn't too crowded. Lester spotted his two new employees quickly. They sat in a corner booth toward the back.

"Gentleman," Lester greeted while shaking each of their hands. "This is the boss lady. The woman whose life you're about to put before your own for the next year."

Neither one of them said a word, just nodded and extended a hand toward Laney. She shook both of their hands and motioned for everyone to sit as she scooted into the booth herself.

"Both of you give me your stories," she instructed with a straight face. "Not the short version either. Make it a little lengthy for me. I have a little time to invest tonight. I need to know who I'm letting into my fold."

The dark, slim one went first. His salt and pepper beard gave away the fact that he was older. "You can just call me Craig. This is my nephew, Debo," he introduced smoothly. He had an uptown accent, like one of those old school gangsters.

Debo looked at Laney and smirked sinisterly as he nodded once.

He was a hefty guy that obviously had a sense of style about himself because he was wearing that Robin Jean jacket outfit he had on. Shit like that didn't go unnoticed with

Laney. Murk had taught her to pay attention to everything, especially the small things. That was why she had locked eyes with him for the longest. He had that scary gloss in his eyes, like shiny pits.

"We some real deal roughnecks from Queens. Ask whoever you want to about us and they'll tell you the same. I have a crew for extra muscle, but I raised this big ass nigga here from the bottle, and he's the only person in this world I trust, so that's why I only brought him along for this job and not a third man. There's no job too dirty for us as long as we're fed."

Laney nodded her head. "Keep going.... That was on the surface. I'm going to need you to get deeper." She put her elbows on the table and sat her face in her hands.

"I have a girlfriend with a wife on the side, and I love those bitches with every fiber of my being, but I can't choose between the two, so I keep 'em both. I been out of prison for a year and still haven't been able to save a dime. I mean, we get money on our own, but it's hard trying to run it up without taking down an armored truck. Which is what I went to prison for in the first place. Let's see, what else... I want to open up a strip club with a daycare in the basement. Shit like that... Debo, tell her about yourself."

"Unk is a bad muthafucka, but I'm the *worst*," he stated simply before sitting back and taking a deep breath.

Craig shrugged, showing his pearly whites. "He don't talk too much. But yeeaahh, that's us. You'll be well protected with us on your squad."

Laney was impressed and entertained by their charisma. She liked their vibe and the fact that they were family. They seemed like stand-up men, and that was hard to find in most niggas these days, so she would take a leap of faith. She trusted Lester with her life, so if he vetted them and thought that they were the right men for the job, then that was what it would be.

"This isn't a squad. It's a family... Which is why I'm careful about who I let in so please don't let me down. I wish to remain untouched, so just keep a bitch protected, and I'll make sure y'all eat like beasts are supposed to. You both going to make two thousand a week on top of your cuts from any side hustles I put you on. Then, you have certain benefits that I offer, but we'll get into those details later on down the line at the end of your beginning contracts next year. Benefits are for career employees only."

"Show us where to sign, Boss Lady," Craig insisted seriously.

Chapter 21

The next day, J-Rock was at a mini golf course outside of a bar and grill, enjoying his afternoon. He invited Tory to join him, so they could chop it up. "I'm feeling that bitch, my nigga. She different than them bougie bitches."

"All this money we got coming in, and you talking to me about a bitch, bro?" Tory asked disappointedly from the sidelines.

"Bitch, that's your job to manage the money. Me, on the other hand, can spend my time doing whatever the fuck I want, and I want that Russian bitch, dawg. That bitch is different. I'm telling you." J-Rock said those last words with passion before hitting the golf ball down the course. He missed the hole by two feet.

Tory shook his head. "Well, get the bitch then, bruh... Anyway, back to the business at hand. It's about that time to pay Big Ant a visit now. That'll be a real power play right there. He got dat car show shit this weekend anyway."

"Factsss!" J-Rock agreed enthusiastically. "I'm going to bring Vanya too... Kill both birds with one bullet."

"Let me run a background on this bitch," Tory decided audibly.

J-Rock gave him a look. "You ain't did that yet, nigga? That's crazyyy."

"How was I supposed to know you would get hypnotized by the bitch?"

"Hypnotize these nuts," J-Rock spat before taking another swing at the golf ball.

****

Laney took Mini out on a shopping spree for last minute things before she had to leave. She had so much shit that she had to have most of her things delivered to the LA mansion from Fed Ex. Mini was going full diva status, and Laney happily sponsored. She never had a problem when it came to investing into Mini.

"I wired you seventy-five thousand into your account, so you'll have some spending money," Laney informed from across the table in the food court.

Mini smiled. "You're so cute when you're being the perfect mom... Thank youuuu!"

"You don't have to thank me for that, baby, but you can thank me for him."

Mini followed her eyes and spotted a fine, bright, clean-cut man strolling up to their table. "Is this him?"

"Yuuuuuup, bitch. I did that," Laney answered while nodding her satisfaction.

Mini quickly stood up, so she could greet her new fine ass shadow. "How old are you?"

"Twenty-seven, ma'am," he answered in a deep voice with a prize-winning smile.

Mini shook her head disapprovingly. "Lose the ma'am. My name is Boss Lady to you... You know karate or something?"

"I'm a second-degree black belt in karate and MMA. I grew up in my father's karate class, and I've also grew up in the mean streets of the west side... If someone tries to harm you, I'm going to break 'em down faster than a dry weed bud," he informed confidently.

Mini's smile was back. "I'll take him," she said to Laney as if they were buying a slave or something.

Chapter 22

Raleigh, North Carolina was one of the few major cities in the state. It was run by a squad called Million Dollar Niggas. If you asked anybody from Raleigh about a group of niggas, they'd bring up the Million Dollar Niggas. There was about a hundred members in the squad, and every last one of them were flamboyant and flashy.

They were known for blowing money like they printed it. Which they actually did. They were some of the best counterfeiters on the east coast. They were so good that you could find some of their bills in a bank safe in just about every major city in the country. Only ten people actually had the recipe on how to cook the cash. Everybody else in the squad moved the money.

It was a magical empire that fed hundreds of families. Thousands of people reaped benefits off of the MDN empire, and they all had Big Ant to thank for that. Big Ant looked after his people, and for that, people of all ages praised him like a god all throughout the city.

That day, he was hosting the sixth annual MDN winter car show on a huge stretch of country grass land he owned just outside of the city. Get money niggas from all over the state showed up to their notorious car shows to flex their muscle. That was mostly at the summer car show though, but hundreds of people still showed up to the winter event. It was basically a Raleigh event.

Big Ant lounged in a lawn chair that was set up on the roof of his pearl white G-Wagon. He was dressed in all white, looking like Big Bank Black on the movie *Super Fly*, down to the shiny white bubble coat and all. He drank out of a bottle of Ace of Spades as he bobbed his head slowly to the blasting music.

He took in the beautiful scene. His people were enjoying themselves, and life was good for everyone. They were a family, and they took care of each other. Everybody ate.

"Daddyyy! Look!" his ten-year-old daughter yelled from down below, sitting on her pink mini four-wheeler.

She pointed down toward the other end of the land, toward the road where a swarm of trucks, cars, and motorcycles made their way up the property toward the cul-de-sac where the event was set up.

"What the fuck?!" Ant spat as he stood up on his roof with a confused expression.

He knew it wasn't his people because *everyone* was there. These were outsiders, and that was unusual. Outsiders usually showed up at the summer car show. As the outsiders made their way down the property, the Million Dollar Niggas began to migrate to the front, and the women and kids migrated to the back as instructed.

"What the hell you waiting on? An invitation? Take her to the back with the rest of the kids," he told his baby's mother before climbing off of his truck and making his way toward the front line with his champagne bottle still in hand.

The intruders began to hop out of their vehicles with all kinds of automatic rifles. Ant's heart began to speed up when he saw Tory hop out of the driver's seat of a black Lamborghini truck. "What the fuck do these niggas want?" he asked no one in particular.

"I don't know, but that's a lot of fucking firepower," one of his captains answered with his 9mm in his hand.

J-Rock took his time stepping out of the backseat of the Lamborghini. He closed the door behind himself and made his way toward Ant. His army approached the meeting point with him. J-Rock stopped in his tracks and so did his soldiers. He motioned for them to stay put and continued to advance forward solo. Ant caught the gesture and did the same.

"All you had to do was call ahead, big dawg. I would've laid out the green carpet for you," Ant informed as the distance closed between the two.

"The only place I call ahead to is the bank, nigga... I'm here as a friend, but it's up to you if we stay friends," J-Rock responded seriously. His good eye stared deep into Ant's.

Ant displayed a look of pure confusion. "I don't got no smoke with you, homie. I show love every time you're in my city, and I check in with you personally every time I'm in your city. So, for you to be pulling up on me like this is crazy."

"Good, so if you're not against me, then you're with me. Rrrighttt?"

Ant nodded his head up and down rapidly. "I'm not against you, my nigga. I always respected you."

J-Rock nodded himself while playing with his goatee. "Okay, so you won't have a problem with committing MDN up under Rock Nation, right?"

"Woahhh," Ant said with wide eyes. "Where is all this coming from? I have my kingdom, and you have yours. We're two hours and thirty minutes apart. It doesn't make sense to me."

"But it does make sense if you smart like me, nigga," J-Rock informed matter-of-factly. "I already run the largest city in North Carolina. This is the second biggest city, and I'm ready to expand, so you either merge your kingdom with mines or I take your shit."

"War ain't good for nobody, J, and I rather avoid it, but I got an army just like you, my nigga. I never been on the bullshit, but I don't got a problem protecting what's mines," Ant warned with his chest poked out.

91

"I'll be generous and say you got about a smooth forty soldiers that will stand up in action and get active for real. Even with outside help, it'll be difficult because you never know how we coming at you. I don't have to worry about how you coming because nobody's dumb enough to come to my city on the bullshit."

Ant didn't respond right away, so J-Rock continued. "I laterally have a hundred die-hard soldiers behind me that will gladly kill, or die, for the cause. Ten of 'em is women, and they more vicious than the niggas. If I let them loose in your city with one of my generals running point, you're going to have some *real* problems. And even if you do hold your ground, which I deeply doubt, I'll send a hundred more niggas... It's simple math, Ant. You win with me, and you lose against me. I'll have you killed — and every other head that grows on MDN — until I get what I want."

Ant was running about ten different scenarios in his head at the moment. He hated it, but J-Rock was right. Rock Nation would crush MDN in a street war. J-Rock was a warlord, and Ant was a finesser. Their armies were reflections of them. See, people rarely told stories about J-Rock. They famously told stories about his many victims and how he literally ran over people that didn't hop on his train.

"What does a merger with Rock Nation look like for me?" Any asked curiously.

"It looks safe, my dawg. You'll be doing a million times better than you would without the nation."

Ant chuckled involuntarily. "I won't even lie. You one helluva nigga... You can tell the wolves to put the guns up. This is a family event, and the kids is getting scared. We'll discuss the details another time."

"Tory was telling me you was going to do the right thing. Looks like he got good judgement, huh?"

Ant shrugged his shoulders. "I guess."

"Check it out. I'm going to Miami for a couple days, but I'm going to leave one of my generals and twenty-five soldiers to deal with the other gangs you been paying because all that is my money now."

Ant's eyes got wide. "Twenty-five? That's it? You need to leave at least fifty. It's four whole gangs I pay to stay out of our lane."

"My twenty-five with your thirty will do just fine. Shit's about to get messy, so anybody who isn't ready to kill needs to be out of sight until the smoke clears. Enjoy yourselves today but tomorrow, y'all need to evacuate. Shit about to get real out here."

Ant's heart accelerated when J-Rock said that last sentence. He was so calm and confident that Ant felt secure that he would come out on top of it all.

Chapter 23

J-Rock took Vanya and ten soldiers to Miami with him. Tory led the army back to the base, so he could get back to work on the business.

It was four in the morning in Miami when they landed. J-Rock rented a brown Ferrari and two black SUVs for the soldiers. They checked into the Kimpton EPIC Hotel on Biscayne Blvd Way. It was a lavish five-star hotel that J-Rock had got accustomed to whenever he was in town.

"I hate flying, but I didn't have the patience for no damn road trip. Plus, I know you wasn't trying to be in the back of that truck for all those hours," he told Vanya as they entered the suite.

She looked over at him and smiled. "Aww, look at the big bad wolf being all considerate."

"Shut yo' ass up!" he spat jokingly, but it came out serious.

"This place is nice... Looks like a nice ass apartment," she complimented, making her way straight to the wall length window to check out the view.

"This my favorite part about the place... Best view in the whole fucking city," he assured as he walked up behind her, stopping just short of contact.

She could feel him close behind her. "I can clearly see that." She turned around to face him. "You don't bring a girl to a place this nice unless you're trying to impress her... I'm getting there."

J-Rock smirked sinisterly before pulling her closer to him.

****

Laney used to love playing up under Murk, and Murk didn't mind because she always made herself an asset in one way or another. On this particular day, they were riding around, smoking and collecting J-Rock's money. Murk had to rough a couple of dudes up earlier that day who had come up short, but other than that, the day was nice and smooth.

A light rain fell constantly that day, and Laney was looking out of the passenger window in her own head. "I think we should start doing our own thing because I doubt we're going to get rich anytime soon by roughing people up and collecting money for J-Rock. My club money is good, but our bills are adding up. Something got to give because I refuse to go backwards. I'm not going broke ever again in this lifetime."

Murk gave her a sideways glance. "You trying to get us killed?"

"Baby, why would he kill us if you're going to be giving him his cut? He'll be glad that you're stepping up, bringing food to the table. He's showing you special treatment and giving you extra responsibility for a reason. He obviously sees something in you so prove him right. What type of nigga do you want to show him that you are? The nigga that asks before he takes what he wants or the nigga that takes what he wants then explains why he did it later?"

Murk didn't answer right away. Future's song, If You Knew What it Took, played lightly in the background as he tossed her words around his head. She actually made sense. "What you got in mind?"

"I mean, it's a few bitches that have been playing up under me at the club, so I'm about to put they ass to work... We can head out of state and seduce some ballers. Get close

to them, find out what needs to be found out, so you and your boys can do what y'all do best."

Murk dipped into a Shell gas station that was just up ahead, swerved in front of an air pump, and slammed the car in park. He rested his arm on his headrest and got closer to her. "You serious right now? That's dirty work right there."

"Hell yeah I'm serious... To the point where I'll pull it off without your help if I have to, Murk. I wasn't playing when I said what I said. I'm trying to live comfortably. I already struggled enough for a lifetime and so have you. If we in this together, it's time for us to start taking risks together," she exclaimed sternly while staring into his pretty eyes seriously.

Murk smirked at her and released a small chuckle. "We is in this together. You see I brought you into my world. I just never knew my way of life would rub off on you so much."

"I don't want to get old and regret all the chances I didn't take at my age now... It's not going to be a constant thing though. If everything goes as planned, we probably won't have to do this any more than five times. After that, I'll have enough money to kick in the next phase of my plan."

"Oh, you got a whole lil' plan, huh?" he asked with a raised brow. "Looks like we got a lot of talking to do tonight."

"Yeah, we'll talk all about that while you rubbing my damn feet because, babayyy, I need it."

Laney snapped back into the present. It was a cold February day at five in the morning on a Sunday. She laid comfortably in her bed, getting rest, but she couldn't sleep even though her night was long. She hadn't been to sleep since the day before, but still she laid there wide awake. She thought back on her past and all the bold choices she made as a youngin. She had a gangster ass past that very few knew about. Murk had turned her into a monster at one point.

It seemed like a whole lifetime ago, back when her and Murk were like Bonnie and Clyde for real. They ended up being a power couple and did very good together up until

Static took her up under his wing. Murk took it the wrong way and ended up having a baby on her, so she dropped him and focused fully on her empire after that until she stumbled across Zion on Facebook.

This wasn't exactly how she mapped her future turning out by the age of twenty-seven, but she was a living legend with a major legacy living inside of Mini and her puppies. She was just slipping into the worry-free stage of her life until she found out about the investigation. After that, there was a lot of mornings like this where she couldn't sleep, just laid up in her own thoughts.

Today felt weird though. Mini was on her way across the country, and Laney was alone for the first time in a long time. She felt sad about it, but on the other hand, she was glad to get Mini out of harm's way. Now, she could just focus on the task at hand — putting an end to J-Rock's reign. She had more confidence than ever and prepared herself to do what needed to be done, but with J-Rock being who he was, it gave her so much anxiety. It was very difficult to deal with.

STANDING ON HER BUSINESS | DG SANTANA

Chapter 24

Tory made it back to the city and got straight back into it. His whole life purpose had become dedicated to keeping Rock Nation above float in every way, and that was a super fulltime position. He had to keep seven gang leaders and multiple businessowners in check. That, on top of keeping up with the money, was a lot, but he juggled it well. He was the hardest working general of them all. That was why he had the highest rank and got paid the most.

His first order of business was to meet up with Murk. Murk was on the east side of town at a kids' basketball tournament that he sponsored every year. He made it clear that he wouldn't be leaving anytime soon, so Tory headed his way.

The basketball tournament was in a park. The sun shined hard, but it was still a chilly morning out there, so Tory grabbed his trench coat to put on over his hoodie.

"It's a lot of people out here, make sure that lil' nigga stay on point. One more fuck up out of him and his ass is off of my security detail. The only reason he even got this last chance is because that's your lil' brother," he said while looking up at his righthand man, Choppa.

Choppa looked back at his little brother, who was now approaching them, and back down at Tory. "I got you, bruh. Everything smooth."

"Aight." Tory led the way toward the event.

The park was live for it to only be ten in the morning. They had a whole DJ and two mega grills fired up.

"Where Murk at?" he asked a youngin he noticed from around the way.

The youngin pointed to a tent on the other side of the bleachers behind the DJ's booth before walking off.

"These folks out here turnt the fuck up this morning," Tory said to himself as he walked past the bleachers where the crowd was loudly cheering for the teenagers on the court.

Tory took the hood from off of his head, so the Vultures could see who he was clearly. They noticed Tory and allowed him to walk into the tent that Murk had set up like a man cave. They sat on blowup couches and chairs while smoking and playing 2K16 on a projector screen. Tory recognized some of the men but none of the women. Knowing Murk, they were from out of town somewhere.

"We betting $500 a game. You trying to get in rotation?" Murk asked him without taking his eyes off the screen. His thumbs moved like a machine on the controller.

Tory shook his head. "Nah, I got shit to do, bruh. Let me holla at you real fast."

Murk released a deep breath before pausing the game and standing up into a stretch. "Aaagggghhhh!"

They stepped away from the tent, a couple of yards into the field, where they could talk privately. "What you need, T?"

"Everything going smooth with the Raleigh takeover. Now, you need to take the Vultures and head to Greensboro and do the same. I'm going to get twenty soldiers to ride with you," Tory informed. He could've easily deployed fifty soldiers, but he didn't like Murk.

They didn't like each other.

"As long as they out of Glock Gang, it's cool because I don't trust them BBG niggas," Murk said, knowing that Tory used to be BBG before J-Rock recruited him into the Nation.

Tory looked up at Murk with a grimace. "How you not trust our oldest ally? You trippin,' bruh... Glock Gang on the verge of getting swallowed up if you ask me."

"I got my reasons. You probably don't see it because y'all the same kind, but them niggas is slimy as fuck, and I just can't trust 'em. And you can say what you want about Glock Gang, but them young niggas standing they ground like a muthafucka. They might be the youngest and smallest gang, but they making they presence known and demanding respect. We made it to where a gang isn't official in this city unless we stamp them. They got stamped, and that shit take heart to do what they doing against the odds. I'm rooting for them," Murk informed defiantly. He absolutely loved a good underdog.

Tory shrugged. "That's on you. Take whoever you want, just get the job done... Find the biggest organization in Greensboro and swallow it up."

"Expansion does make a lot of sense right now... Consider it done. I'll head out tomorrow morning."

"Nah, nigga. J-Rock said immediately, so you'll be headed out tonight and on the job in the morning."

Murk clenched his teeth. "Like I said, I'm heading out in the morning. If J-Rock got a problem with that, he can tell me himself," he retorted before walking off, back to his tent.

Tory mugged him nastily as he walked off. You would never be able to tell that he and Murk used to be close friends back in their juvenile days. Prison and distance turned them into strangers, and by the time they were reunited in Rock Nation, they didn't mix well. They didn't get along, not even a little bit. Tory felt like Murk considered himself special to everyone else, and Murk felt like Tory was an ass kisser to J-Rock. They both had their own perceptions.

"Did I hear that nigga say he don't trust BBG?" Choppa asked once he made his way over to Tory. They were both from the west side where BBG was born.

Tory nodded slowly. "Yuppp. Nigga ain't got no muthafuckin' respect. Talking about he don't want no BBG soldiers and he want Glock Gang behind him."

"He always had nuts though. You can't even take that from his ass," Choppa said with a shrug.

"And that's going to be his downfall. Watch this," Tory promised before leading the way back to his car.

Chapter 25

Laney was having an ordinary day up until someone knocked on her door. She answered the door and was met by a parade of purple balloons and flowers.

"Special delivery for you, ma'am," the chubby, white delivery man announced before handing her a large purple card.

She stepped aside, so he could carry the balloons and flowers into her apartment. She stood there with a wide smile as she read the card.

This is just to let you know that you are loved, missed, and greatly appreciated. I know I'm difficult and my situation is difficult, but you never gave up on a nigga, and I thank you so much for that. You the perfect bitch for me. You the light in my tunnel, and I wouldn't trade you for shit in this world. I'm going to get out of this muthafucka and cater to your lil' ass. Until then, just keep your faith in us. We going to prosper fasho. You my sexy mama 4L!!!!

She thanked the delivery guy before closing the door behind him. "Look at all this shit." Zion had outdone himself once again. There were five sets of flower boxes and about twenty mega balloons with different purple heart themes.

Even from prison, he still made his presence felt, and she loved it. It was the small shit that mattered the most with her. She hoped he never changed that about himself.

"Now you know you didn't have to buy me all of this shit, babe. I loveeeee it though! Thank you, Daddy!" she greeted once Zion answered the phone.

"You welcome, sexy... How was your night?" he asked curiously.

Ever since she stopped filtering her life to him, he'd been asking a lot of questions, but she didn't get annoyed by it because he was her man and had her best interest at heart.

"My night was decent. We made some good money, and my new operation is finally up and running. Them clients was going crazy without my puppies," she joked seriously.

"I bet... You got them hoes working that witchcraft on them niggas. That's why," Zion joked back. "Nah, but how is the new bodyguards doing?"

"They're alright. Lester's still training them, but they're some solid dudes. They should be a perfect fit," she predicted.

"That's what I like to hear... You trying to watch this movie with me?"

A bright smile grew on her face. Those words were like music to her ears. "You damn right, nigga. Let me go get my lil' fire stick," she added playfully.

Their situation wasn't ideal, but they made the best out of it together. All that mattered was that they both made each other's life better.

****

Vanya was enjoying herself more than she thought she should've. J-Rock wasn't that easy on the eyes, but his demeanor was so sexy to her. Then, there was the fact that they were actually getting along so well. Everybody made him seem like a monster, but to her, he was just another man who wanted a woman to understand him — a woman like her.

103

"Why don't you expand out here? That way, you'll have an excuse to fly out here. This shit is beautiful," she thought verbally, how he'd been encouraging her to do.

The sun was barely up, and it was a pretty chilly morning. It was too chilly for them to hop in the water, so they just slowly walked the shoreline of the beach barefoot, so they could feel the cool sand.

"I get the picture you trying to paint, but North Carolina is enough of a headache for me. I'll let Florida be someone else's headache," he explained. "Why don't you just quit your job and come work for me? You'll be making twice as much, and the job comes with benefits."

She smiled and rolled her eyes. "It seems like you're trying to suck me up into your world until I can't find my way out. You strike me as that type."

"I'm the type to take risks when I get a gut feeling... This is that, baby girl," he informed matter-of-factly.

"I'm a therapist. What kind of work do yon have for me?" she asked curiously as her pretty, black, linen dress flopped in the sudden breeze of wind.

"You can count money and even invest some of it for me if you're up for it."

She stopped in her tracks. "Are you serious right now? Like really serious?"

J-Rock nodded with a straight face. "Do I strike you as the type of nigga that plays? I see something in you that I like for real, and I'm trying to show you that."

"What's the catch?" she asked before starting to walk again.

"Ain't no catch. As long as you be loyal to me and never cross me, I promise you won't remember what it feels like to worry about a muthafuckin' thing... You seem to be well informed about me, so you should know how I handle disloyalty, so yeah, once again, don't cross me."

"You'll be surprised at how loyal I could be," she responded surely.

Chapter 26

The basketball tournament was turnt up to the max. There were first, second, and third place prizes issued to the winners of the fifteen teams that participated — $2,000 cash to each player on the first-place team, mini motorcycles to the second-place team, and brand-new iPad minis for the third-place team.

Murk got together with a few OGs from around the way a few years ago, who were giving back to the community, and hopped on board. They were standup men, and they were for their people, so Murk associated himself with them from then on.

After leaving the tournament that evening, Murk snatched two Vultures and made his way to Glock City. Glock City was Glock Gang's only territory in the city, but they held it down like a fort. Glock City consisted of five ten-story apartment buildings that sat in the same complex. Their advantage was the hill that the complex sat up on and the woods that surrounded it all.

Murk drove his Ferrari down the road that swerved through the woods on the way up to Glock City. His Vultures followed close behind in a Dodge Charger.

The apartment complex had a gate surrounding it, but the entrance gate stayed open. The security booth was empty, and Murk knew exactly why. Nobody in their right mind wanted to work security in Glock City. It was public news what happened to the last security guards, so people just stopped applying for the job. Glock governed the land, and that was that.

The apartments were run by a rugged bunch of renegade teenagers, and they put fear in niggas twice their age. They were stronger than Tory and the rest of the gangs gave them credit for. They were barely fifty deep but were surviving two active wars and got a seat at Rock Nation's table. Murk had been in the shadows studying them the entire time, and he felt like now was the perfect time to swoop down on them.

By the time Murk made it to the heart of the complex where the large recreational area sat, young niggas had emerged like roaches on a garage floor, surrounding the two vehicles that were now parked on what used to be a tennis court.

Murk opened up the driver's door to the red Ferrari, and a super thick cloud of weed smoke could be seen escaping the vehicle up under the beaming streetlamps that lit the complex up. He stepped out comfortably and adjusted his black jean jacket, unfazed by the wolves that surrounded them. His Vultures had exited their vehicle as well and made their way over to Murk's side.

"You just better have some good family out here!" one of them shouted.

"One of y'all lil' niggas tell Glock that Murk Da Vulture out here for him!"

They stopped in their tracks at the mention of the name, only a few feet away by now.

"Follow me," one of the youngins instructed after getting off of the phone.

Murk was escorted all the way up onto the roof of the building at the back of the complex. There was a mega tent set up on the middle of the roof. "You can go inside, but these niggas got to stay out here with me."

Murk respected it and dipped into the tent solo. Glock lounged on a black leather couch comfortably with his head resting on a pretty young lady's lap as she played in his long, thick box braids. He was on his back though, so he eyed Murk as he made his way into the tent.

"You got a hard ass set up in this muthafucka. I got to get me one of these tents," Murk complimented genuinely. He really had a thing for tents.

Glock sat up with the sigh of a forty-year-old man. He was stocky but a little on the chubby side, and the lack of exercise was hurting his breathing. He waved the girl off, signaling her to get out of the tent, then he gave Murk an impressive expressionless stare after she was gone. "What you want, bruh? My dues paid, and I'm staying out of the way. Tell J-Rock I can't help that all these niggas hating on the kid."

Murk helped himself to a seat on the other end of the couch. "I'm not here for J-Rock. I'm here because I see something in Glock Gang. I'm one of the few niggas that actually likes you, lil' nigga... The choice is up to you, but under my wing, it'll be a different ball game."

"Under your wing? Why the hell would I do that? I'm nineteen, and I already got a seat at the table. I'm a whole mayor in Rock Nation. I'm straight, bruh," Glock retorted matter-of-factly.

Murk shook his head in disagreement. "Don't let your pride get in the way of a good decision, young nigga. I see a lot of myself in you, so of course I understand how you feeling, but it don't have to be Glock against the world. Everybody needs allies, bruh, and trust me when I say I'm the ally you need. The vice president. The other gangs won't fuck with you if Glock Gang is under my wing. That way, you can focus on getting to the money. I know you trying to get rich, young nigga. That gangsta clout ain't going to move your mamma out of these bricks."

Glock clenched his teeth and stared off into the distance. Everyone knew of Murk and how much weight and fear the Vultures held in the city. The more he thought about it, the more sense it made. Murk stood on the same principles as himself, and the Vultures were good examples for Glock Gang.

"We would be dangerous as fuck together. That's a fool ass team. Niggas going to be shook," Glock stated with an evil smirk on his handsome baby face.

"Definitely not going to be a force to be fucked with but fuck these niggas. Don't get caught up in that shit. Got to focus on building a better future for yourself and these lil' niggas that's following you," Murk advised.

Glock nodded. "I hear you, bruh... What now?"

"Now, you come to Greensboro with me, so we can handle some business for J-Rock and get this money in the process. I'm about to show you how to work around the system."

"Just me and you?"

"Hell nah... Bring your best ten shooters. Y'all about to glide with the Vultures. Teach y'all a thing or two," Murk informed coolly.

He had a secure feeling when it came to his decision. Glock Gang was Vulture material, so they were untouchable now.

Chapter 27

Two days later, J-Rock returned to his kingdom. He had a damn good time with Vanya and enjoyed himself more than usual on the trip, but he still itched to get back to the grind. After dropping Vanya off, he headed straight to his house, so he could shower and head back out to show his face around town.

"You're much bigger in person," a woman's voice said from the distance.

J-Rock didn't jump, but his head snapped over into the dining room where he laid eyes on the sexy Hispanic woman that sat on the table, gazing at him carefully. Two armed men had their pistols trained on him. They stood on either side of her.

It took J-Rock a moment to respond verbally. He couldn't believe someone had the balls to break into his shit. He was honestly more confused than anything else.

"My name is Karmen... I'm Fernando's previous handler and your current handler... Since you executed my last employee, you have to do the job for them. Look at that stolen shipment as a bonus for the job," she informed seriously.

"So, what about Armondo?" J-Rock asked with squinted eyes. "He not going to try and get no get back for his folks? I'm just going to get rid of him just in case."

"You *will* *not* make any advances on Armondo's life at all. He's a retired man now and is out of the game, but he understands the game. Fernando's time was up in the game, and there was no better way for him to go out than a blaze of glory." She hopped off the pool table and made her way over to him in the living room. "Do we have a deal?"

"How many bricks can I buy?" he asked curiously.

"For every five hundred you buy, we credit you two hundred fifty. There is no limit on the quantity of bricks. You get as many as you can buy. Fourteen thousand each."

He looked down at her and rubbed his hands together in prayer position. "We got us a deal." He extended his hand for a shake.

She sealed the deal with her hand into his.

****

Laney sat on the couch in her office and counted her personal safe deposits from this week. She had just come back from the bank, depositing last week's income for the lounge, and now she had to clear the other safe in her office. It came out to just under twenty thousand dollars. That was her cut from all the side action that took place in the lounge. She capitalized like a muthafucka off of her position and was excited to see Mini do the same for herself.

"So, niggas really pay to come in here and shoot music videos, huh? This place is a fucking goldmine," Craig stated with enthusiasm. He stood at Laney's window and peered down at the video shoot taking place. "That shit is fly, son."

"Yeah, the lounge is a goldmine if you want to be real about it," Laney schooled. "She puts food on everybody's plate, so in return, we take care of her very well."

Craig laughed lightly. "So, the lounge is a broad now, huh? You're wild, Boss Lady."

"I guess... Debo! What's up, nigga? You really don't say shit, huh? A bitch forgot you was in the room," she shouted even though Debo was just right there across the office.

"I bite more than I bark," Debo retorted matter-of-factly through a sinister smirk.

Laney just shook her head. "Shit, that's fine with me."

"Your cooks make seafood down there?" Craig asked while rubbing his stomach under his Pelle Pelle jacket.

"Yeah, but no crab. Just lobster, shrimp, fish, and oysters."

Craig assured his return before sliding out of the office, more than likely to get closer to the action downstairs.

"Looks like it's just you and me, big fella," she said to Debo before getting up to put the money into her purse on top of her desk.

Knock! Knock!

Someone knocked lightly on her door.

"Come in!" she instructed immediately. It was more than likely one of her girls.

One of her waitresses stuck her head in. "Uhmm, Boss Lady. That chocolate man who always wears a suit is here, and he says he needs to talk to you now."

"Okay, tell him I'll be right down," Laney instructed before taking her Gucci slides off to put on her heels.

After checking herself in the mirror for blemishes, she headed out. "Let's go, big guy." Debo got up and stalked behind her.

"Mr. Manning, *please* tell me something good today. I'm having a good day. Let's keep it that way," she greeted once she was in Mr. Manning's section.

"Depends on how you look at it... I finally cracked my source and got her to talking. Speaking of, you owe me ten thousand dollars too because I had to pay her right then and there... Long story short, she's a senior agent for the FBI and can get you immunity if you give them J-Rock. All you'll have to do is get him to admit that he's the leader of Rock Nation on recording, and they'll wrap their entire case around that. You won't see a day in jail."

Laney took a deep breath and ran a manicured hand down her face.

Chapter 28

In Greensboro, a king named Nardo had been murdered, and Travis took his spot. The crown was just as heavy as Travis had expected, so he was prepared for what came with it. He had to maintain order within his kingdom and protect it. His organization was big on structure, so order wasn't the problem. The problem was protecting his kingdom.

Four days ago, Nardo was kidnapped after leaving his favorite local strip joint. The two men he was with were killed in the parking lot where Nardo was snatched. The one witness who saw the crime didn't have her contact lenses in that day, so she wasn't very much help to the police or Travis.

For six long hours after Nardo's abduction, Travis didn't know what to think. For six long years, no one opposed the organization. They'd built an airtight system and put the city on their backs. Most people loved Nardo, and he had very few enemies, so Travis couldn't make sense of it until a video was sent to his phone of Nardo being tortured. He was asked to kneel to Rock Nation and denied.

He stood his ground and died on his feet. He was a solid nigga to the very end, and that made Travis want to go that much harder for him. J-Rock had life fucked up if he thought he was going to bulldoze his way into Greensboro. Travis had mad respect in the streets, and his replacement as the new king was accepted by the heads of the local gangs. That was all the ammo he needed.

Travis beefed up on security and had all the gangs on high alert for any oncoming threats. He had all his bases covered.

"Nigga going to definitely stop smoking this weed until we kill the threat. Shit got me paranoid as fuck," Red stated seriously. He was one of those slick light skinned niggas. He was more into the money aspect of the game than anything. Everything else was just shit that came with it.

"Speak for yourself, nigga," Travis retorted. "That shit keep me calm."

Before Red could respond, Murk and Glock walked through the sliding door to Travis' backyard. "Oh, y'all out here watching the news on the projector? That's a first. Actually kind of playa given the current situation," Murk stated casually as he made his way around the pool, toward the sitting area.

Glock stalked up behind him with his pistol trained on them both, the green beam playing ping pong on their bodies. "Move, I'll put you in a shit bag," he promised sturdily.

"You J-Rock?" Travis asked Murk, trying to hide the fear in his eyes and figure out how the hell they found his girlfriend's house. Nobody but Red and himself knew about it.

"Nahhh, nigga, but he sent me. The Vulture," Murk answered.

Travis took one look over at Red, and when he averted his eyes. Travis knew what it was. "You slimy ass nigga!"

"You was trying to get us killed fast. You must've didn't watch the same video I saw. Just do the right thing and hear these folks out," Red suggested desperately. Travis had them in a tight spot.

"Man, fuck that. They need to hear me out. I helped build..." Travis was cut short by three hallows to the torso from Glock's pistol.

Red looked up at Murk with wide eyes.

"What? Shit, we just did you a favor. He would've killed you," Murk said matter-of-factly.

Red just shook his head and looked over at his now lifeless friend. "How the fuck did this happen? Shit was all good just a week ago."

"We going to rebuild with you as the head of the organization. From what I hear, you a get money nigga, so that's what you focus on. I'll handle the rest," Murk instructed.

"What's *the rest?*" Red asked curiously.

"Asking too many questions will have you looking like your mans right there," Murk threatened before walking back toward the house.

Glock stood there a little longer, looking at Red's patheticness. He chuckled and shook his head before spinning on his heels into a jog, so he could catch up with Murk.

****

Laney walked into the prison's visitation area, looking like a short ass model. She always stepped out, especially when she went to go see her man, but she showed her ass on this particular visit.

Zion stood there, looking at her through wide eyes, as he waited for her to make it into his awaiting arms. "Damn, girl, you look like a fucking angel. Smell like one too," he whispered into her ear as they hugged before the long kiss.

"Thank you, baby. I'm feeling good today. All this wickedness will be behind me soon, and I can move on with my life. I'll be able to focus on our relationship more, and we can be great again." She painted a picture with her words.

The words brought comfort to Zion as she spoke them. He'd been so worried about her wellbeing lately and upset that he wasn't able to be any real help to her. "Oh, yeah? I don't even need no details or nothing. I'm just glad you got some good news because I don't like how much yo' ass been stressing lately. You been trying to hide it from me, but I know you better than you think."

Laney rolled her eyes. "Whatever, nigga. I'm just glad I'm going to be able to be a regular girlfriend to you again."

"Yeah, me too. I'm not even going to lie. I love dat role on you. You adorable as hell playing it," he admitted with an intoxicating smirk. "It's going to be difficult when I get out, but we going to make it work."

She gave him a suspicious look. "What the hell you mean by that?"

"Calm down. I'm just talking about how you going to want a nigga to sit back, but I'm trying to hit the ground running."

"Really?" she said before releasing a sigh. "I'm just trying to keep your hardheaded ass out of prison. Soon as those BBG niggas get their hands on you, you're going to be back flipping bricks in no time. The prices just dropped in the city too, shiddd!"

Zion shook his head in disagreement. "I told you I'm not fucking with the soft no more, and I meant that. I will be moving a fuck load of weed though," he joked seriously.

Laney stood up out of her chair. "I'm about to go get you some food, nigga."

"Don't forget my Fritos!" he called after her.

"Shut up, nigga. I know what you want," she snapped back, making the supervising female officer laugh.

Zion sat there and admired his woman. She looked so delicate but was more solid than most niggas he knew. He felt like he had won a prize with her, and he didn't like it because he wasn't used to it. He was used to being the catch, but Laney was in a league of her own. She was different in every type of way.

Chapter 29

After the visit with Zion, Laney met up with Vanya in a Walmart parking lot. The industry's high traffic provided good cover for their quick meet.

"It is way too cold today," Vanya complained after getting into the passenger's seat of Laney's vehicle. "I promise this'll be the last time I step foot outside today."

"I wish I had that luxury. My empire won't run itself... Anyway, I have some good news," Laney informed with a smile.

Vanya raised her brows.

"Your mission is almost over. All this shit is about to be behind us."

Vanya squinted her eyes. "Sooo, you found a way to get him out of the way?"

"And did!" Laney answered sassily. "My source just let me know that the Feds are trying to cut a deal with me. They'll give me immunity and scrap the whole investigation if we can get some recordings of J-Rock admitting that he's the head of Rock Nation."

"Oh, yeah? So, you want me to plant some listening devices in his car or something?" Vanya asked nervously. Her heart rate began to rise just by the thought.

Laney shook her head with her nose turned up. "I mean, that would be the easy thing to do, the smart thing to do, but I guess I'm not all that smart because I just can't bring myself to do that shit."

"So, how in the hell is that good news then?"

"I never said that was the good news. The good news is that even though I'm not going to cooperate with the Feds, all this is still going to be over with."

"How?" Vanya asked skeptically. "You going to have him killed?"

Laney nodded slowly with a stone-cold expression etched on her face.

****

Glock watched with wide eyes as Murk stabbed a man for the second time in his last good eye. "Now, you laying there screaming like a bitch. That's on you. All you had to do was tell me what I want to know."

The man didn't respond. He just kept screaming at the top of his lungs in agony, so Glock put him out of his misery with a single bullet to the head. The screaming was killing him. He'd heard men scream before from a bullet but never like that.

"And then there was two," Murk announced with the knife pointed at the other two young men who were tied up in the garage.

"Man, tell that crazy ass nigga what he want to know!" one of them said to the other.

Murk smiled and bent down in front of the skinny man. "So, you got the answers I need, huh?"

"Man, I overheard my uncle say that they hold everything in the three-story house by the railroad. The one next to Dollar General."

Murk looked up at Swiss and gave him the nod. "Go check it out. Take five Vultures and ten of the youngins."

"For your sake, I hope you not playing games. I'm going to make your death real slow if you are," he promised before wiping his knife off on the boy's shirt.

He stood up and faced Glock. "You trying to play the game until they come back?"

Glock stood there with his hands by his side and his braids tucked into the hoodie he had pulled over his head. He looked into Murk's grey eyes and sensed nothing. The nigga wasn't at all fazed by what he had done. "I always heard you was a crazy ass nigga coming up, but to see this shit up close is different. You need counseling, bruh."

"You spend three years on J-Rock's security detail and see how you come up out of that shit," said Murk seriously while walking away toward the entrance of the house they had just confiscated.

Glock just shook his head and followed. He didn't normally follow niggas, which was why he made his own gang instead of joining one, but Murk was a different type of nigga. He was probably the only nigga that Glock had ever met worthy of him looking up to. J-Rock was a vicious muthafucka, but he was an idol for Murk's generation. However, very young menace coming up these days followed in Murk's footsteps. Murk was the idol for Glock's generation.

An hour and some change later, Swiss returned with every single soldier he had left with. "Shit checked out. It was like seven niggas there, so we had to get active, but we flanked 'em from behind and got the best of 'em. It was a stash house though. We got three trash bags full of pills and two duffle bags with money in them. It's all in the trunk of my truck."

Murk nodded slowly in satisfaction. "Okayyyy! Now, that's a good lick right there."

"You going to let us live?" the heavyset boy asked desperately while looking up at Murk with pleading eyes.

Murk nodded. "Yup. I'm a lot of things, and a man of my word is definitely one of them," he said before leading the way out of the house.

Chapter 30

Lester paced the floor of the lounge. Craig and Debo sat there comfortably. It was early in the day, so the place was basically empty except for staff that was preparing for the evening.

"Okay, this is going to be a big boy mission. Some top secret ass shit we're about to have to pull off."

"Yeah, tell me about it. Boss Lady want us to pull a miracle," Craig agreed. "Wouldn't it be easier if she just had the Russian bitch slip the nigga some poison?"

Lester stopped and nodded his shiny, bald head rapidly. "Of course it would. That's the first thing I suggested, but Laney don't want to put too much on her or chance that she'll choke or not. Killing a man is no small thing."

"Let's get this shit over with," Debo urged irritably.

Lester gave Debo a strange look.

"He's just excited," Craig informed. "What you got in mind though? How we going to approach this?"

Lester went back to pacing. "That's the tricky part right there. Usually, I would just take the nigga out with a sniper from about a hundred yards and start rumors in the streets about how it was the Feds that sent the hit, but we can't go that route."

"Why?" Craig asked as he clasped both hands together.

"It has to look like a natural death. Apparently, the city will go up in flames if the Almighty J-Rock is killed in cold blood," said Lester.

Craig shot him a blank stare before releasing a chuckle. "Yeah, I'm going to leave that up to you. If you need somebody beat to death, stabbed, or shot, holler at us."

Debo nodded his head in agreement.

****

Once he triple checked the daily income for the Nation, Tory hopped in his mud green Jeep Trackhawk and headed to his neighborhood. It had been a couple of months since he slummed it in the field with the soldiers, and he was feeling the urge, so he told his security detail to meet him there.

SandHurst Apartments was one of the most feared hoods on the westside, and Tory was like a god in his hood. He might've devoted his life to Rock Nation, but BBG was in his blood, and everyone knew it. They loved him for it. He never turned his back on his people.

Word spread quickly of Tory's appearance, and it brought the whole westside out to SandHurst. Dope boys and killers, kids and women. It turned into a celebration. Old school and new school cars flooded the field behind the apartments. Old heads brought the grills out, and the vibe was just pure.

Tory hopped out of his Jeep and paused. He had a wide-legged stance as he took in a slow and deep breath. If you let him tell it, his hood had a unique smell of its own. That, mixed with the food smell and all the smiles from his people, made a perfect welcome home for a gangsta. He dove into the action and mixed in with the crowd.

"See how we lay the red carpet out every time for yo' Black ass?" Big Body noted. They could pass for brothers. Big Body was just taller and chubbier.

Big Body and Tory used to be K-Drop's top enforcers for all of BBG. They were fiercely loyal to him until Big Body had a falling out with K-Drop. BBG split into two for weeks until Big Body caught up with K-Drop and executed him publicly. Big Body grabbed the reigns to BBG and was the reason why Tory got drafted to J-Rock's security detail. Four long years later, and they were still soaring.

Tory looked around at all the action and smiled his ugly smile. "Y'all do act up when it come to the kid. That's love right there... What's up with Nitro though? He look like he about to catch a heart attack over there."

Big Body looked over at the commotion on the side of an apartment building and shrugged his shoulders. "Shit, I don't know. Let's go see."

A little semicircle was formed around Nitro as he ranted, using his hands for better effects. He was one of those extra messy ass niggas. Tory shook his head as they approached. As much as he was a piece of shit, he was manipulative, which was how he became a sergeant in BBG. They never got along too well, but the respect was between them.

"What's going on?" Big Body asked curiously as they neared.

All eyes were on Nitro. None of the other soldiers said a word.

"A lil' situation. I got it covered though, big dawg. Just some lil' petty shit," Nitro assured dismissively. "Matter of fact, I'm getting these niggas ready to go handle that now," he informed before walking off with the soldiers close behind.

"I swear I never trusted that nigga there," Tory admitted.

Big Body shook his head in disapproval. "You need to stop your shit... Anyways, what's new in The Nation?" he asked before leading the way over to one of the food tables.

"That nigga, Murk, can't be trusted. He linked up with Glock," Tory informed with a bad taste in his mouth. He couldn't stand the little disrespectful muthafucka.

Big Body shrugged nonchalantly. "Shit, they're both crazy as fuck. I can see them getting along... Matter of fact, now that I think about it, they're perfect for each other."

"You not looking at the bigger picture, bruh. The Vultures and Glock Gang is a dangerous mix. I know Murk. He's going to turn them young niggas into deadly weapons — weapons that will be a threat to us," Tory predicted sourly.

Big Body cut his eyes at Tory suspiciously. "You acting like we at a full-scale war with them niggas. Yeah, we sent a few blitzes at each other as a test of strength, but that's just the game. They still eat off the same table we do, my nigga. Glock made that happen despite everything we threw at the lil' nigga. Let him be. If Murk want to snatch the young nigga up, that's good for him. As long as they stay off the west side with that shit, then we're good."

Tory nodded his understanding but didn't say a word. Big Body had his hands full with BBG, so he was blind to a lot of shit outside of that. Tory was in a higher position on the board, so he viewed shit even Big Body couldn't. Murk and Glock were no good together.

Chapter 31

Meanwhile, in Manchester maximum security prison, Zion stood at the window in the front of his housing unit, watching his young nigga lay game on a decent female officer as they walked down the walkway together, like they were taking a stroll in the park.

He turned around and faced the dorm. A bunch of misery, anger, and depression shoved into a metal can. Most niggas did drugs to mask it, but Zion had been gone long enough to see through it all. He grew extremely observant over the years, and he used his militancy to his advantage. Which was why he was in his current position.

He chuckled suddenly, drawing weird stares from a group of niggas who stood by him. He caught the stares but didn't pay them any attention. A few years from now, they would understand.

"You got that look in your eyes, my nigga." His main partner, Yanno, pointed out as he approached the window.

Zion smirked sinisterly. "Fuck I tell you 'bout watching me?"

"You know don't shit get past me, nigga... You ready for this journey?"

Zion nodded his head slowly with a satisfied expression etched on his face. "Hell yeah I'm ready, nigga. I been locked up for eight long ass, hard ass years. It's time to take off like a rocket, bruh."

"And I'm going to be in this bitch rooting for you every step of the way." He had a life sentence that he was still fighting.

"And I'm going to stay in touch like I promised, nigga," Zion promised before Yanno walked off to go handle his business.

Zion considered Yanno to be family and would hold him down through the storm. He just had to get himself right first though before he could help anyone else. God was giving him a second chance at life, and he planned on making the absolute best of it. He just had to get over this one last hump, and the rest of his life was smooth sailing from there.

He could taste the peaceful freedom.

****

Laney was in tremendous shape naturally, but she still hit the gym up every now and then, just to tone her body up. Whenever she did go to the gym, she went hard. She had been in there for two hours, bouncing from station to station.

Usually, she would be complaining to herself and panting for air by now, but on this particular afternoon, she was intensely focused. She had psyched herself out and had just taken all of her current frustrations out on the workout.

All types of thoughts surfed around her mind. It amazed her how life still gave her anxiety after everything that she had been through in her life. She should be just as cold as J-Rock and Murk at this point of her life, but she knew she had a beautiful soul and refused to kill it, so she just suffered silently.

She reached down and pressed a button on the treadmill that made it go faster. She started to run faster as if she could rum from all of her problems.

"Hello." She answered her phone through her AirPods and slowed the treadmill down to a speed walk.

"I got a solid plan for the funeral," Lester informed in code since they were on the phone.

Adrenaline began to course through Laney's body, to the point where she had to turn the treadmill off and take a seat on it. The realization of what she was about to do became that much realer. She was about to send a hit on the most powerful man in the city. The entire state.

The smart side of her brain was telling her to run to her attorney and take the deal, but the real nigga in her spirit wouldn't let her go out like that. J-Rock had to die, and that was that.

"Uhmm... Hellooo! You hear me?" Lester asked urgently.

Laney snapped back to reality. "Damn, my bad... Meet me in my garage in two hours because I'm at the gym and have to get dressed still. I have dinner with Karmen at her place."

Two hours and thirty minutes later, Laney met up with Lester and got in the backseat of her truck. Craig and Debo followed behind in Lester's Chevy pickup.

"So, what you came up with?" Laney asked curiously.

"My buddy from the service used to sleep with this medicine lady out there in Taiwan. She specialized in healing but knew all about poisons too. Long story short, there's this flower out there that only grows deep in the forest. It contains a liquid that causes natural-like strokes."

"You got to be shitting me," Laney said skeptically. It sounded like some shit from a spy movie or some shit.

Lester nodded. "I know. I wouldn't have believed the nigga myself if I hadn't met the woman myself all those years back. She's the real deal and so is he. If he says he has some of that poison, he has it. Apparently, he been making a fortune off of it on the dark web."

Laney thought about it for a second. It was the best option she had. A natural death from J-Rock was perfect. No questions and no revenge. Not even Rock Nation could extract revenge on God himself.

"I guess we're going to find out if he's the real deal or not. Call him up. We're about to go all in, bruh. You with me?" she asked with enthusiasm, trying to pump herself up just as much as him. The stakes were higher than Pookie from *New Jack City*.

Lester knew it too, but he still answered for her benefit. "Of course I'm with you."

Chapter 32

Karmen laid out the red carpet for Laney. The young princess had mountains of potential, and Karmen wanted her to see what she saw, but it would take time. It was time that she obviously had hence the fancy dinner date.

She looked at the security monitor on her TV screen. She had her personal hacker mirror the security footage from the building, so she saw exactly what the security guards saw in the control room. She did this same thing everywhere she went. When you'd been in the game as long as she had, extreme precautions became wise.

"The girl knows how to dress. I give her that," she complimented as she watched Laney strutting through the lobby with her little entourage in tow.

She rocked a short, black, leather jacket with leather, thigh high boots to match. She carried herself royally, and that was why Karmen embraced her to the extent she was. She'd done some homework on Laney and was genuinely surprised by the feedback. She was a female legend and equally respected by both men and women.

"I might have to move in this building after all. I love the hell out of this layout. It might be worth the extra cash," Laney said when Karmen answered the door.

Karmen stepped aside, so she could walk in. "This building is elegant. It's my first time staying here... How have things been going though?"

"According to the plans for the most part," Laney answered truthfully. "I just try to keep myself busy, so I won't overthink shit."

"Overthinking can be something like a superpower if you learn how to filter it right," Karmen schooled as she motioned for Laney to take a seat at the fully prepared dining room table.

Laney gave her a skeptical look before taking a seat at one end of the long table. "Speak for yourself. I'm trying to get over this hump before a bitch goes crazy."

"Believe it or not, you're dealing with adversity better than most women would. You especially surprised me when you turned down that deal from the Feds. It was a sweet deal. They're desperate for J-Rock at this point. They have far less evidence than they're letting on."

Laney gave her a confused look.

"What, you think you're the only one with eyes and ears around the way? Honey, my security is *very* thorough, so when I embraced you, they began to keep tabs on you and did a deep dive into your past. I'm impressed to be honest. You go take what's yours and don't wait for anyone to give it to you," Karmen noted.

Laney looked at her through squinted eyes. She could see clearly between the long lashes. "What exactly do you want from me?"

"Believe it or not, I really just want to see you prosper. I see a lot of myself in you. You thrived in a big man's world, just like me. That's no small thing right there. Lately, I've been becoming bigger on women empowerment, especially women like yourself that's in the game."

Karmen felt close to Mini, and she didn't think it was just a coincidence. It was about time she started a legacy of her own since she couldn't have kids, and that legacy would start with Laney. She didn't know it yet, but Karmen had big plans for her.

****

After leaving Karmen's spot, Laney headed to Target to go meet Vanya to give her a rundown about Lester's plan to take out J-Rock. She thought about what Karmen said about the investigation and everything else she said.

Laney needed that dinner with Karmen more than she ever knew. They built with one another, and Karmen dropped a ton of jewels onto her. She soaked up all the game she could and even proceeded to write some of it down into the note app on her phone.

After that, she responded to a sweet and lengthy message from Zion. It warmed her heart because she was just thinking about how she missed the effort he put in to make her day, and there he was. It was like he had heard her soul crying out for his affection or something.

"This muthafucka is extra packed." Lester pointed out. "They must be having a special sale today or something."

Laney looked up from her phone. "Yeah, I didn't know they had all this going on. I would've chose another meeting spot."

"I mean, it is more cover. She still ain't going to have trouble finding your truck. Ain't too many grey Maserati trucks in the city," he assured.

Laney shot Vanya a text and let her know that she was parked toward the south entrance of the parking lot. Five minutes later, Vanya was walking up to her truck on feet. She had to park somewhere else because the place was packed.

"Girl, you wearing that peacoat," Laney complimented as she climbed into the back with her.

Vanya shivered a little, thankful for the heat that blew in the truck. "Thank you," she said as she reached for the phone in her coat pocket.

"Who's that? Ta'Jae?" Laney asked before putting the phone up to her ear. "Hello."

"You a bold bitch, bruh. I swear I ain't know you had it in you. I mean, you set some niggas up to get robbed with Murk, but to take a shot at the king over ratting me out. That's some gangsta shit right there," J-Rock admitted intensely.

Laney's eyes grew large, and her adrenaline spiked. "What the fuck?! Bitch, you triple crossed me? Ta'Jae put you up to this?" she spat at Vanya.

Lester turned around in his seat. "What's going on?"

"Nah, she don't belong to Ta'Jae no more. She the first lady of Rock Nation, believe it or not. She belongs to me," he informed matter-of-factly.

"Oh, shit!" Lester shouted once he noticed that they were being surrounded by men from all directions.

"Sound like my soldiers closing in on y'all asses. You played the game, and you lost."

Lester looked over and saw that Craig and Debo were already being held at gunpoint with their hands up. The rest of the men stood surrounding the Maserati with their guns out. "Damn!"

Laney didn't know how to feel. Her whole world had just been wrecked, just that fast. "Just please leave Mini alone. She has nothing to do with this life," she pleaded as a single tear ran down her face.

She had the natural urge to burst out into a full sob, but she didn't want to give J-Rock the satisfaction, so she kept it gangsta until the very end because she chose this life. She tried to get out, but it didn't look like she would be that fortunate.

"She won't be touched if you get out of the car and follow my soldiers, so they can bring you to me," he reasoned before ending the call.

Laney took the phone from her face and launched it straight at Vanya's face with surprising force.

131

"Ouuwww! Stoppp!" Vanya screamed and pleaded as Laney rained hard punches down onto her face. The two rings she wore on her punching hand didn't help at all.

Shit was starting to get real bloody in that backseat, so Lester had to pull her off of Vanya into the passenger seat. Laney had an urge to climb back there and hop right back on that ass, but she just caught her breath for a second.

"You don't understand. He's the best man I've ever met. We're in love with each other!" Vanya explained from the backseat while balled up on the floor in a fetal position.

"Bitch, say another word and I'll kill you my damn self. That's on my daughter," Laney barked viciously.

Lester stared at Laney through wide eyes. He knew she came from the streets, but he didn't know she was a fucking savage. This must've been what she meant all this time when she applauded herself on coming a long way.

"I got to go, bruh. If you don't hear from me by the end of the night, you know what it is," Laney instructed seriously. She avoided eye contact, not wanting him to see the rage.

Lester's face twisted up badly. "You know you got me fucked up. I'm coming with you... He probably want to torture you and all type of shit. If that's the case, we might as well shoot this shit out right now!"

Laney shook her head in disagreement. "It'll be worth it if it mean the safety of my daughter. He threatened her once, and I don't take that lightly. If I die today, promise me you'll look after Mini like you do for me."

"Damn, man!" Lester spat as he pounded the steering wheel out of frustration. His heart was breaking, and he wanted to lash out in his own fit of rage, but it wouldn't help anything.

There would be no smooth verbal farewell between them, so Laney just leaned over to place a quick kiss on his cheek before getting out of the truck.

Chapter 33

Laney was loaded into the back of a minivan and just sat quietly as she was driven to her last destination. Her entire life was replaying in her head as she wondered if she'd go to heaven or hell. She thought of Zion and Mini, who'd definitely be crushed by her death the most.

She had left her phone in her purse in the backseat of her truck, but it probably was for the best because she really didn't know what to say to them. She just didn't know anything right at that moment. All that she was sure of if that would be her last day on this earth was that J-Rock had checkmated her ass. She had lost and had to pay with her life.

Twenty short minutes later, they were pulling up to one of Rock Nation's most common meeting spots. It was a church on the north side of town. J-Rock took the church over once the pastor ended up owing him a huge debt from gambling. The church provided many services for Rock Nation over the years.

Laney was escorted into the church where she was met by familiar faces — J-Rock, Murk, Tory, the other four generals, and the five leaders of the gangs that ran the city. They all had eyes on her. The blood on her beige trench coat gave her a distinct appearance — that and the grimace on her face.

"What the fuck is she doing here?" Murk asked urgently. In his mind, he knew what it was, but he didn't want to believe it.

"That, my nigga, is a solid ass bitch. That's what she's doing here," J-Rock answered matter-of-factly.

"I don't get it," Tory added with a curious expression. J-Rock couldn't stand Laney's guts, so something was off.

Laney was escorted to the front row where everyone lounged. Laney wasn't worried about everyone else. She had her eyes trained on J-Rock. She wasn't expecting spectators, but J-Rock was petty like that, so she wasn't surprised.

"Y'all meet the new chief of staff. She's going to take charge in my absence. I'm gonna go lay low in Jamaica with my cousin, so I can take over Kingston," he informed to everyone's surprise.

Everyone, including Laney, was openmouthed as they looked up at J-Rock up on the stage. He had just dropped two humongous bombs on them. And he didn't play about Rock Nation, so everyone knew he was deathly serious.

"Wait, what?" Tory said with a twisted face. "What the fuck did you just say?"

"Y'all heard what the fuck I said. Now, shut the fuck up so I can explain... North Carolina is our stronghold in America, and I'm trying to make Rock Nation global, so I'm going to start in Kingston, Jamaica then on to the next city. I want Rock Nation in as many countries as I can. Plus, it give me a chance to expand my horizon."

Murk shook his head. "You been watching too much *Fast & Furious,* bruh. We don't need Rock Nation in another country. This the best country in the world."

"And what happens when this country turns its back on us? We need to have connections and allies in other countries. Anyway, my decisions are final. I just got everybody together, so it could be heard from the horse's mouth," said J-Rock.

Tory took a deep breath. "Aye, y'all get up out of here. We got it from here," he commanded.

The generals and the gang leaders didn't waste any time vacating the church. None of them wanted to be in the middle of their inside family drama.

"How the fuck you just going to drop bombs on us like that? You leaving? This bitch the chief of staff?" Tory asked frustratedly.

"Yeah, that's crazy. Even for you, bruh," Murk agreed.

Tory nodded in agreement with Murk.

J-Rock applauded them with a few claps of his large hands. "It's good to see y'all bitch ass niggas agreeing on some shit for a change. Y'all need to keep that shit up while I'm gone... Yeah, I chose Laney to be in charge because she clearly has what the fuck it takes to hold shit down. She more dangerous and ruthless than y'all niggas think, so I advise y'all not to undermine or underestimate her. As far as me leaving, y'all will understand as time passes."

"What you got to say, *Boss Lady*?" Tory asked Laney, heavy on the sarcasm.

Laney shot him a death stare. "Nigga, I ain't ask for this shit, so take that up with your big homie and shut the fuck up talking to me."

"Woah, woah, woahhh! Y'all three are going to be the brains, muscle, and heart of The Nation. I'm going to need y'all to set your differences aside and keep my legacy intact, or I'm coming back, and *I swearrrr* y'all don't want that," J-Rock stated very seriously.

He hopped down off of the stage and began to take off his black, Givenchy, trench coat, leaving him in a matching turtleneck sweater that displayed his muscular physique. "Y'all two get the fuck out. I got to holler at Laney one-on-one for a minute."

Tory and Murk left without any other words because they clearly wouldn't make a difference. J-Rock had made up his mind, and that was that.

"I thought you were going to kill me," Laney admitted. Her breaths were still short though due to her anxiety.

J-Rock shook his head and pointed over toward the seats where she stood. "Nahhh, you're more useful alive to me. Why kill you when I could just give you a life sentence in Rock Nation? I know how bad you wanted out of the underworld, so me burying you in the bottom of it is enough torture for you. And that's enough satisfaction for me."

"I swear I fucking hate you. Always have and always will," she admitted again with a slight cringe.

J-Rock shrugged his broad shoulders nonchalantly as he stood directly in front of her, smirking down at her. "That's alright as long as you respect this shit... Now, your job to is keep shit in line and keep everything operational. I'm going to introduce you to the plug before I leave next week, and you can take it from there."

"I'm not cut out for that shit, and you know it," she warned. "You setting a bitch up for failure."

"You tried to have *me* killed versus snitching on me for immunity. That's some gangsta ass shit right there, girl. You more equipped for the position than you know."

"Whatever, man. You sparing my life. I guess it has to come with a price," she reasoned with a shrug.

J-Rock pointed his index finger in the air, like he had just remembered something of great importance. "Oh, yeah, one more thing."

"What?" Laney asked curiously. There was no telling what J-Rock would say out of his mouth this time.

To her surprise, it wasn't a word he dished out. It was a forceful blow to her face. J-Rock backhanded her so hard that she flew back onto the bench behind her. "Vanya's the first lady of Rock Nation now. Don't you *ever* put your hands on her again."

She sat there, holding her face, as he retrieved his coat and made his way out of the church. "I'll be in touch with you though! You got the keys now. The city is yours!" His voice echoed through the high ceilings as he neared the exit.

Laney just continued to sit there long after everyone was gone. She held her pulsating face and stared up at the giant cross hanging up on the wall behind the stage. It was backgrounded by lighting to give it a more holy look.

"God, please look after a bitch. Looks like I got a long and bumpy, road ahead of me."

Chapter 34

Laney looked at herself in the bathroom mirror as she made sure her makeup and everything else was on point. The white linen lingerie set she wore was extra sexy. She had carried herself like a straight goddess the whole weekend, and the man she was there to seduce treated her accordingly.

Woo was a bigtime dope boy in Virginia at the time, and he met Laney at a car show in Miami a few months ago. He knew her as Nessa from Memphis, Tennessee though. It was one of her many fake identities for her licks, and Woo was clearly a whale.

This was her third time in his personal mansion just outside of Richmond, Virginia. He was even more tender than she'd expected, and after she put the pussy on him, his soul was hers. He was so giving and into her that she decided not to even rob the nigga. She'd get more out of him if she played the long game, and that was exactly what she was doing.

She stepped out of the bathroom and grabbed her titties while sticking her tongue out at Woo playfully as she made her way to join him in the big bed. He smiled at her while showing the deep dimples of his fat face but went back to his conversation. Laney got in the bed and picked up the iPad, so she could continue her online shopping spree.

"Nigga, that's three million dollars' worth of dope. You ain't about to have your lil' cousin watch it. Your ass going

to watch it until everybody come pick up what they supposed to get," he commanded seriously.

He sat there with a twisted face, but it softened after a while. "Damn, I ain't know it was about your mama. Alright, go ahead and head to the hospital, nigga. I'm on my way there now. I'll watch it myself because I don't trust them new niggas you hired to package."

Woo hung up the phone and looked at Laney. "I'll be back a lil' later, bae. This mandatory business right here." He was already out of the bed, putting on his T-shirt.

"Man, I might as well just head back home to Memphis. Every time I come over here, you find a reason to leave a bitch in this big ass house by my damn self. I didn't fly all the way out here just to be alone, Woo," she complained in agitation.

"You don't want to be in that house with them stink ass drugs," he warned.

She shrugged. "If you can take it, so can I."

Like always, Laney got her way. Woo brought her with him to the stash house. After complaining to him about how uncomfortable Woo's workers made her feel, she got Woo to send all four of them home.

Ten minutes after they were gone, she went into the bathroom. She stood in the mirror, looking at herself harder than she'd ever done. She took a deep breath and stormed out of the bathroom, down the hall, and into the living room.

"Bae, you got to watch this movie with me," Woo suggested once he heard her coming up behind him.

He didn't hear her flip the kitchen knife in her hand and bring it down hard into the side of his neck. To Laney's surprise, he jumped up onto his feet and turned around to face her with wide, angry eyes. He had one hand on the knife in his neck and the other outstretched toward her as he made his way around the couch to get his hands on her.

"Ohh, shit-shit-shit!" she spat alarmingly as she fearfully backpedaled toward the kitchen.

Woo moved like a big ass zombie as he stumbled forward, trying to catch her. She tripped and fell but still got back up onto her feet before he could catch her. She ran into the kitchen for another knife, a bigger knife. Once she grabbed the knife and turned around, he was right there.

His thick, sausage hand was already wrapped tightly around her neck, trying to choke the life out of her. He probably would've succeeded too if she hadn't been stabbing him repeatedly in the stomach with the bigger knife. His grip eventually loosened around her neck, and he slowly fell down to the floor where he took his last bloody breath.

Laney dropped the knife and frantically wiped her bloody hands on the front of her white halter top repeatedly, like she was trying to wipe the sin off. Her stomach was in her ass, and she was dizzy. Without a warning from her body to her brain, she bent down and vomited on Woo, making the scene look that much more gruesome.

Her nerves was shot, and she was basically shaking at that point. She had to remind herself to breathe. She just wanted to ball up in a corner somewhere, but she had come too far now. She had to see her decision through, so she spent a few moments pulling herself together and got straight to business.

She loaded all ten duffle bags into his Mercedes then started a fire in the house, burning all the evidence. After leaving the stash house, she headed back to his house to erase any existence of herself. It took her six hours and three bottles of bleach to clean the house, but she got it done.

She disposed of her clothes, showered, and changed. Without a breath or an ounce of sleep, she hopped back into his Benz and drove four straight hours back to Charlotte. Her mind was racing, but she had Drake's Take Care album on replay. For some reason, it just calmed her down at the moment, so she just went with it.

When she got back to the city, she went straight to the apartment she was sharing with Murk on the west side. "Get up, nigga!"

Murk popped up with the quickness and clutched his pistol in the same motion. He was a light sleeper. "What you doing back so early?"

"Here. You got work to do so get your ass up," she said after tossing him the keys to Woo's Benz.

Murk caught the key and examined it curiously.

"It's ten duffle bags in the trunk and backseat. I don't know if it's coke, or heroin, or fucking meth. I just know it's worth three million. My advice is for you to sell it outside of the city, so we won't have to break J-Rock off, but however you do it, I still want $750,000 off of it. I don't want to wait until it's all gone before you pay me, I want my fucking money asap, Murk. Not in payments, all at one fucking time. I just got blood on my hands for them drugs. I'm not doing that shit ever again."

Murk sat up in the bed, looking at her, openmouthed. "Damnnnn, you murked the nigga? I thought you wasn't going to lick him."

"Babe, I wasn't planning to, but he got too comfortable with me, and it cost him. I didn't want to kill him, but it was the only way. If I could've, I would've called you, but you wouldn't have gotten there in time, so a bitch had to handle the business. Now, it's on you to do your part. Go sell them damn drugs!" she commanded urgently.

Murk couldn't even say shit. He just got his ass up and got dressed before jogging out of the house with his gun in one hand and car keys in the other.

After he was gone, Laney flopped down on the bed and stared at the ceiling. With her cut of the drugs, she would be able to go legit how she'd always dreamed of. She had a shot at a real life, and that gave her some sort of comfort. She would be able to put her shady present behind her and do something meaningful for a change.

Chapter 35

Laney thought about that day eight years ago when she'd put her demons behind her. The greedy cutthroat bitch that she felt herself turning into at the tender age of twenty was laid to rest that day, and she had vowed to never go back to that person. Current circumstances threatened that vow she'd made to herself. It was like she was in a high stakes dice game with the devil himself.

"I'm telling you, Laney, you going to have to show everybody your strength. Tonight gives you the perfect opportunity to do that shit. The only thing these niggas respect is evil. If you want everybody to respect you, that's the only way," Tory pleaded with her.

J-Rock had a long talk with Tory before he left and painted the bigger picture for him. Laney would be the brains, Tory the heart, and Murk the muscle. Together, they had to keep the legacy going, and failure wasn't an option. J-Rock had babysat them enough, basically raised them all in one way or another, and had very high expectations of them.

"You sound just like Murk's dumb ass. I'm not killing them folks. Y'all do it," Laney spat with a quick roll of her eyes. "Niggas know wassup with me. I'm in this spot for a reason."

Tory shook his head. "Nah, fuck all that shit. That's not enough... You about to walk in that muthafucka and shoot them niggas in they heads one-by-one. I'm telling you. If you don't show these niggas that you ruthless, somebody going to kill you eventually. All type of plots behind your back. This organization is run off of fear."

"Alright, man, goddamn! Let's go," she commanded frustratedly before he led the way into the rundown house on the west side.

Soldiers of all ages lounged around on the ground level of the house, but only the politicians were allowed in the basement. Big Body and Ice waited on them as they made their way down the basement stairs.

Ice was an albino pretty boy ass nigga, who was the leader of Swipe Gang. They were a crew of scammers, who made big bucks. They were stamped Rock Nation and were supposed to be protected, so when it came to light that three BBG soldiers were behind a robbery on a few Swipe Gang members, Ice called for heads, especially since one of the victims ended up dead.

Laney nodded at them both. "These the niggas that did it?"

"Yeah... I already know the rules, and they apply to everybody, even me, but I'm not killing my own soldiers, and you know his bitch ass ain't going to do it," Big Body spat, referring to Ice.

Ice twisted his face up. "When you getting money like me, lil' nigga, you'll know what it feel like to never have to lift a finger... It's levels to this shit."

"Nigga, I'm moving a hundred blocks a month," Big Body countered matter-of-factly.

"That's not all your money, nigga. You got more mouths to feed than..." Ice stopped mid-sentence when he saw the black hunting knife that Laney pulled out of her purse.

She stormed over to where the three men were tied up in chairs, walked up behind them, and individually slit each of their throats swiftly. It was like she'd done it many times before.

"Any other problems before I head back downtown?" Laney asked them while wiping the blade of her knife off on one of their shoulders.

Everyone shook their heads no, but no one said a word. She had no doubt turned every man on in the room. You only saw bad bitches like Laney do shit like that on the TV screens. The grey, skintight, Palm Angels sweatsuit she sported only intensified the whole moment.

"Tory, you need to be focused on getting those bricks out there to Jamaica safely. J-Rock's looking forward to that shipment, so you need to be all on top of that shit... Body, walk me to my car," she instructed after replacing her knife in her MCM purse.

Big Body followed her up the stairs and out the house. He walked her to her truck and stood outside as she sat in the backseat, facing him with the door open. "I'm going to need you to keep your dogs on a leash. Shit like that can't be happening. Swipe Gang pay us good money to be left alone. Shit like that falls on you, my nigga."

Big Body gave her a hard stare before speaking. "I know. That's on me. It won't happen again, Boss Lady."

"Kill that shit with Glock Gang too. We're all in this together. We got our hands full with these other cities until we can trust them new niggas. Plus, we got to focus on getting all this damn work sold. That should be the main fucking focus around this muthafucka!" she reminded with dread.

He nodded his head and turned his fitted cap to the back. "That's already handled. I got you. You can count on me to pull my weight. Just ask J-Rock."

"J-Rock's not coming back anytime soon, nigga. We stuck with each other. We got to build our own bond. Just show me what you made of," she challenged before closing the door on him.

As Lester pulled out of the driveway, Laney sat back in her seat and took a deep breath. "Stop the truck!"

"What happened?" Lester asked urgently after slamming on the brakes.

She rolled down her window and waved Big Body over. He was still standing in the same spot, smoking a freshly lit joint of weed. He walked over to her window. "What you need?"

"That shit ain't laced, is it?" she asked him, pointing at the backwood.

He gave her a knowing look. "I don't fuck around like that. You just snapped."

"Shit, I got to ask... Let me get it though. See what y'all weed talking about out here," she stated before accepting the joint.

"That shit will put an elephant on its ass. Straight from the motherland," he boasted with a smirk.

Laney hit the weed lightly, so she wouldn't cough, and rolled the window back up. "Let's go, Lester. Take me home."

"Everything good with you? What happened in there?" Lester asked with clear concern in his voice as he pulled onto the street.

"Yeah, I'm good. Just need to get out of my head," she answered dismissively before taking a series of pulls from the joint.

She commended herself for keeping her shit together in the basement. The way she acted like killing those men didn't faze her was amazing.

"Turn that up," she told Lester once he cut the radio on.

She slouched back in her seat and puffed away at the weed. Before she knew it, her heart rate and her breathing had slowed. She was calm, and the weed had her faded, just how she needed to be at that moment in her life.

As the reality of J-Rock's life sentence kicked in, she smiled. He had ended up being smarter than she gave him credit for. She was worth way more alive, like he said, so giving her a high-ranking spot in Rock Nation bounded her for life. There would be no retirement for her. She was cursed for life.

She began to chuckle to herself again as she thought about it further. Life was a muthafucka fasho.

Chapter 36

Karmen showed up at Laney's spot the next morning with two espressos from Starbucks. "Looks like you had a rough night."

"If only you could imagine," Laney agreed before grabbing one of the Styrofoam cups and leading the way into the condo.

She was hung over from the weed and had a super-strong urge to inhale some more, so she texted Lester and told him to pull up on Big Body and grab a pound for her to smoke on. She looked how she felt. Her hair was all over the place, and the crooked pajama pants didn't help. She plopped down on the couch and took a deep swig of the espresso. It was good.

"How's the throne treating you?" Karmen asked as she took off her peacoat.

Laney gave her a look. "J-Rock can get this muthafucka back."

"I'm not even going to downplay it... J-Rock is far more clever than I ever gave him credit for. He made me a believer. Placing you as the head of Rock Nation in his absence is probably one of the smartest moves he's ever made," Karmen complimented before taking a few sips of her own espresso.

Laney sighed. "I'm still surprised he spared my life. I just knew I was dead, girl. The only reason I didn't break down is because I knew my daughter would be well-off in my absence."

"That's the point I'm making. He's smart... You're going to do just fine. I'm going to make sure of that," Karmen promised. "I see you haven't taken off the chain."

Laney reached up to grab the choker chain that Karmen had gifted her. "You said it was good luck. Looks like I'm going to need as much of that as I can possibly get."

"Yeah, it's blessed... Well, let me get going. I have a flight to catch. I'm off to Chicago for a while. Just wanted to check on you personally before I left. I'm going to keep in touch with you now, so you make sure to do the same. I don't embrace many people like this," Karmen informed before standing up.

"I got you and neither do I," Laney responded matter-of-factly.

About thirty minutes after Karmen had left, Lester was at Laney's front door. "Thank you so much, bruh," she said before reaching to grab the small bookbag out of his hand.

"You're welcome, but do you think you need all that? That's a lot of weed just to be smoking. You going through it like that?" he asked in concern.

She shrugged. "I just know this is what I need at this point in my life. Can't we just leave it at that?"

"Alright... I just been worried about your mental. I'm still learning this version of you. That's all," he informed carefully while watching her on the other couch, examining the buds of weed in the large jar.

"Shit, I got to relearn this version of myself. Just bear with me. My whole life was just flipped upside down. I'm trying to balance all of this shit out."

Lester nodded in understanding. "Like I told and showed you a million times before, I'm here through it all. You saved my life, so I'll forever protect yours."

"I know. I know... Go get you some rest though. We have a long night ahead of us," she suggested while rolling her weed in a Tops white paper.

"Yeah, that's a good idea," he agreed before letting himself out.

Laney fired the joint up and sat back on the couch comfortably. "I guess you're my new sneaky link," she joked as she talked to the weed.

****

Later on that night, Laney schooled Craig on the basics of management. "Just look at it like a car and you're the motor. Keep this bitch running. I've been watching you and how you've been wiggling in the loop on your free time. You have what it takes. I just have to train you a lil' bit."

"So, you're really about to leave me in charge of this place?" he asked, surprised. "I don't want to fuck nothing up."

"You got this. I know you been taking control on my behalf when I'm not around to catch the attention of some celebrities. You going to do just fine. Just keep utilizing your finesse and make sure all my money adds up. Other than that, you can basically freestyle it," she advised before walking over to the mirror to check her appearance.

Someone knocked on her door, and Missy stuck her head in. "Busy?"

"Nah. Let me holler at her real fast, Craig. We'll talk more about this tomorrow night."

Missy and Craig locked eyes as he headed out, and she headed in. "He's cute. How long you plan on having him around?"

"You see he's in my office. He in it til' death now," she joked seriously. "What's up though, baby? What's the problem? Everything good with the girls?"

"Hell yeah. We got the spa doing numbers. I'm running that muthafucka like Ace Boogie," Missy joked with a smile. "I just came to check on you though. I transferred that money to the account you sent me too."

"I'm good, baby. Just making sure the ship doesn't sink, and yeah, I seen it. You been taking on extra responsibility, so I'm going to start paying you more. If you manage your money right and check them spending habits of yours, you'll have enough to buy a nice house."

Missy gave her a knowing look. "I got to buy this lawyer first, Boss Lady. You know that."

"I retained a good paternal lawyer for you yesterday after we talked. So, like I said, work on saving for the house. I'll plug you in with a realtor that won't ask too many questions."

"Oh, my fuckin Godddddd!" Missy screamed as she quickly closed the distance between them, her phat ass jiggling in the bodysuit she sported. "You the realest bitch on this earth. Don't let nobody tell you different."

"I'm only real to those that keep it real with me. You done put in work and held it down, even when it got hard. You never complained over the years, so all that shit paying off for you. You earned your stripes," Laney assured as she pulled away from Missy's embrace.

Missy looked Laney up and down. "You looking real sharp in that pantsuit. That's the new swag, huh? You been killing 'em lately. Make me want to step my game up."

"What you waiting on then? You don't need permission to elevate. You a made woman now, baby. Boss up," Laney encouraged before changing into her designer heels, so she could head out.

Missy nodded her understanding. "Okay, say no more... I'm about to head back to the spa though. I got to keep my eye on those dizzy hoes."

Laney chuckled. "We got a good batch of bitches. They mean well."

"Yeah, I'll die about those bitches fasho. Alright though, just hit me up if you need anything, Boss Lady. I'm gone," Missy said before walking out of the office.

Laney gathered all of her belongings and left her office soon after. Lester and Debo lounged in the hallways outside of her office.

"Big Body say he needs to see you asap," Lester informed as she locked the door behind herself.

"That better not be about that weed. That was a part of his dues," she joked seriously.

Lester shook his head. "Nah, I doubt he gives a fuck about that. It seemed urgent though. I was just about to stick my head in there and let you know. He texted me an address and all."

"Okayyyyy... Take me to him, I guess. Murk can wait," she decided before leading the way out of the lounge.

Chapter 37

Lester took Laney to the address, and they ended up at a mansion not too far from Ta'Jae's palace. It wasn't in the same housing community but definitely in the same vicinity.

Big Body and Tory stood outside in the wraparound driveway, waiting on her, leaning on one of the many luxurious cars parked in front of the mansion.

"What's this all about?" Laney asked them suspiciously once she stepped out of the truck.

Big Body closed her door behind her. "You'll see. It's a special surprise."

"What the fuck you smiling for?" she asked Tory, who sported a creepy smile.

"You'll see," he answered matter-of-factly.

Laney sighed. "Let's just gone in here because y'all niggas is acting weird as hell."

"After you," said Big Body with an outstretched hand.

Laney shook her head and led the way after putting on her jacket.

They were searched at the door by four big, foreign men outside of the front door, then they were granted entrance inside after being confirmed on the list while a party took place. It wasn't the type of party she was used to though. It was a real upscale type of party with a wide variety of people mingling with one another. She also noticed all the different ethnicities in the room.

They dressed professionally and had a real live band playing instruments for them. Big Body, Tory, Lester, and Debo were the only people in the room who had on sneakers and jeans. Nobody seemed to pay them any special attention though.

"What are we doing here, and how the hell we end up on this list?" she asked Big Body and Tory.

"You about to see. The first fight starts in ten minutes," Tory informed before picking up a champagne flute off of a server's tray.

Laney looked around in confusion. She didn't see a boxing ring in sight. She just took a deep breath and went with the flow. If she hadn't been on the weed, she probably would've walked out in agitation. The party was a vibe though, so she stuck around.

They stuck to themselves for the most part, and everyone else basically avoided them, which worked for them because none of them were friendly. Ten minutes passed quickly, and everyone was escorted to the basement where there was a huge metal cage. They were instructed to find a seat in the bleachers by the spokesman.

"I'm proud to introduce you all to the seventy-third Death Tournament. Seventy-three months ago, a powerful group of elitists from all around the world got together and formed the most profitable tournament in the history of tournaments. These fighters are the best of the best around the world, and every one of them have something critical to fight for to make things more interesting! This is our first tournament in North Carolina," the chubby spokesman announced in English, but he had a foreign accent. He looked Middle Eastern.

Laney looked over at Tory, who shrugged and put his attention back on the announcer, who stood by the cage.

"There are four fights taking place tonight... These fights are to the death, and there will be no weapons involved. $250,000 will be awarded to the last man standing from each fight, then the three winners from each fight will be placed back in the cage where they'll do a free-for-all. The last man standing out of the three winners will go home with $750,000 in an untraceable account."

The first two men were introduced as they made their way into the cage. Since the fight was to the death, there was no need for a referee. They were about to fight it out until only one man was breathing.

The fighters warmed up and stretched in separate corners of the cage as spectators placed high stakes bets on the fighters. Some placed cash bets with the bookies, and others wagered on the dark net. The announcer informed that there were nine hundred thousand people streaming the fight from all over the world. It was a five-hundred-million-dollar operation.

Laney sat there, literally stunned. She was openmouthed and stuck. "How long y'all knew about this shit?" she asked Tory.

"Shit, we new to this shit just like you," he answered truthfully.

"So, who the hell invited us to this shit? J-Rock?" she asked curiously.

Tory shook his head. "Nope. You going to see."

Laney sighed and rolled her eyes. She was relieved when she looked over and saw Big Body rolling up some weed. She needed to calm her nerves.

"I'll be right back. I'm about to go place a bet on the bald head nigga," Tory informed before making his way over to the bookie.

Fifteen minutes later, the fight began, and the conservative and uptight partiers that were upstairs turned loud and boisterous. The place turned into a zoo as spectators screamed for blood as the two fighters clashed and battled it out. The bald, Hispanic man was shorter than the tall, white man, but he had more weight. They both were obviously skilled in close combat.

The fight lasted for two long minutes before the bald man caught the white man in the chin with a fierce kick that sent him crashing down to the floor. The bald man quickly got on top of him and finished him off with repeated head blows onto the hard, stone floor under them.

Tory and Big Body were cheering since they had just won some money on the fighter, but Laney, Lester, and Debo just sat there, staring at the gruesome scene.

"This shit is for real," Lester acknowledged audibly.

Laney nodded. "Hell yeah, I can see that," she responded as the cleanup crew cleaned up the body and the blood.

Thirty minutes later, the next two fighters met in the death cage. There was a fat, Russian man and a muscular, white man. That fight only lasted for twenty seconds. The white man snapped the Russian's neck after getting behind him.

Tory and Big Body had chosen another winner and collected their money. They had both made thirty thousand apiece.

"I'm betting the whole thirty racks on this next fight. Fuck it," Tory encouraged.

Big Body shrugged. "Fuck it, all or nothing."

"You might as well get in on the action," Tory suggested to Laney.

Laney gave him a look. "Hell no. That's why y'all brought me out here to bet on this sick ass shit?"

"Nope... That's why we brought you out here," Tory informed while nodding at the announcer, who was setting up to introduce the next fighters.

"This next fighter is a Charlotte native and fresh out of a prison cell. Coming in at two hundred ten pounds, standing at 6 feet even, we have Zionnnnnn!" The crowd cheered as Zion made his way out of the back and into the cage. He only wore training shorts and track sneakers. His hands were already wrapped up, and judging by his face, he meant fucking business. He was a fucking savage, and it showed in his every feature.

155

Laney almost had a fucking heart attack. "Tory, what the fuck is this?! Oh, hell nah! He ain't about to fight in this shit!"

"This shit is out of our hands, Boss Lady. Ain't no going back now. All you can do is provide support right now," Big Body advised.

Laney looked at them with a crumbled face. "So, this was the fuckin' surprise? Y'all knew about this shit?"

"We didn't find out about this shit until it was too late," Tory informed with a shrug. "I'm about to go place these bets though. I got faith in my nigga. I used to go to his boxing matches back in the day. I know what the fuck he can do."

Laney sucked her teeth before popping up out of her seat and running toward the cage with Lester and Debo hot on her tail.

"Zion, what the fuck are you doing? How long have you been out, and why did I have to find out like this?" she spat once she made it to the cage. Her voice cracked after every other word.

Zion slowly rotated his shoulders in his corner of the cage. He looked over at her with intense eyes. "Go back to your seat. I'll explain after I win this tournament," he commanded confidently.

Before Laney could respond, the background lights dimmed, and the spotlight was on the spokesmen. "Our next fighter is all the way from a village in South Africa. Coming in at two hundred fifty-five pounds, standing at 6'5", we have Uwakkiiiiii!"

A big, Black Panther looking ass nigga stalked out from the back and strolled confidently into the cage barefoot. He was cut up like Wolverine and looked like he was raised by apes. His big hands were rough. Everything about him was rough. He was every bit of a fucking warrior.

"Oh, helllll nah! Babe, walk out of that fucking cage now!" she pleaded fearfully. She couldn't watch her soulmate get killed savagely in cold blood.

"Listen, this ain't nothing you back out of. It's something you get through. I made my choice, now I got to see it through," he informed nonchalantly. If he was fazed by his opponent, he did a *tremendous* job of hiding it.

The tournament security approached Laney and informed her that she had to get away from the cage. She took a deep breath and reluctantly made her way back to her seat.

"I told you. You think I ain't try to talk his ass out of this crazy ass shit. He just keeps stressing how it's too late. So, shit, it is what it is at this point. I'm still about to bet on my nigga. Fuck it!" Tory stated before collecting Big Body's money and heading over to the bookie.

Lester grabbed Laney's shaking hands. "He's too calm. If he has that much faith in himself, then so should we. I can understand why he wanted you to be here. His back is against a large wall with another wall closing in from the front, but he has people here that are in his corner no matter what the odds."

Laney took a deep breath and just started praying silently for her man. She didn't think she'd ever been so scared for someone else in all of her life.

Chapter 38

The fifteen-minute betting period had passed by for her too damn fast, and the fight was starting before she knew it. She wanted to turn away and cover her ears, but she had to watch. There was a good chance this would be the last time she saw Zion alive. She had to watch. Zion's pretty, light skinned ass looked so fragile compared to the charcoal giant that he faced.

Zion bounced like a kangaroo, obviously counting on using his speed and mobility to his advantage. It was all he could do. It was clear that Uwakki had the advantage of strength.

Uwakki swung a punch with so much force that it made Laney cringe. Zion ducked it and danced around to the other side of the cage. "Let's go, babyyy!" she shouted defiantly, making sure he could hear her.

Zion did the unexpected and went on the offensive. It was an aggressive approach at that. Uwakki was expecting to be chasing Zion around the cage for most of the fight, so when Zion came straight at him with surprising force of his own, it threw him off. Zion delivered an impressive combo, landing two stiff jabs on Uwakki's big nose.

Uwakki hopped back and shook it off before rushing Zion with a combination of his own. Zion stood his ground and deflected most of the punches, but Uwakki landed a brutal kick on Zion's outer thigh.

Zion took the blow and collided with Uwakki again. He surprised everyone with his aggressive approach. He stood toe to toe with Uwakki as they went blow for blow. Uwakki was obviously stronger and tougher, but Zion possessed more skill and used that to his advantage.

Zion hit him with two mean hooks and swiftly sidestepped to the left, so he could dodge a blow. He caught Uwakki with a quick jab then slid back a pace, just out of reach of another one of Uwakki's blows. He was calm and calculated, but Uwakki, on the other hand, was growing angrier by the second. Zion was beginning to annoy him in a major way.

He got Zion in a corner and rushed him. Zion tried to duck and dodge him, but Uwakki was on it. He grabbed Zion around the waist and sent a brutal knee to his midsection.

Zion doubled over, and Uwakki took the opportunity to body slam him onto the ground, so he could take advantage of him. Zion knew it was life or death, so giving up wasn't an option. He had to find a way out. By then, Uwakki was on top of him, raining punches down. Zion deflected them to the best of his ability.

Zion leaned up a little and sent a crucial punch at Uwakki's balls. Uwakki doubled over, and Zion took the opportunity to go in for the kill. He leaned up and literally bit a nice chunk out of Uwakki's throat. Blood squirted and splashed out of Uwakki's neck as he wrapped both hands around it, trying to stop the blood.

Zion got to his feet and spit Uwakki's flesh out before proceeding to stomping his face in until he was unrecognizable. Zion released a savage-like victory yell. Uwakki's blood ran down his chin and down his neck. Zion was the true warrior of the fight, and Laney was overwhelmed with relief.

"That's seventy racks apiece, bruh!" Tory informed excitedly. "I'm putting the whole thing on Zion for the next match. I know that's going to bring back at least $300,000."

"Shit, me too. I'm all in at this point," Big Body agreed.

Laney shot them a nasty look. "My nigga is out there literally fighting for his life, and y'all worried about some damn money."

"Shit, he's going to be fighting regardless. Might as well bet on his ass." Tory shrugged.

"If he dies, y'all die. How about that?!" she barked seriously before sitting back in her seat and crossing her arms firmly.

Tory and Big Body looked at each other and shook their heads. They couldn't even say anything. She held the power to end their lives if she really wanted.

Thirty minutes later, the free-for-all match had started, and Laney was literally on the edge of her seat. Zion did the smart thing and let the bald Hispanic and the muscular white man clash. He stayed in his corner, studying both of their fighting styles.

The white man dominated the Hispanic easily, knocking him out cold with a clean left hook. He then bent down and snapped the Hispanic's neck. It was obviously his favorite finish move. He stood up and locked eyes with Zion.

"I promise you this shit won't be that easy!" Zion challenged confidently. "I got something for your big ass."

"Let's go, nigger! I'm going to crush you like a little grape!" the white man countered disrespectfully.

Zion jumped up and down in place, exercising his footwork. It was clear that he didn't plan on attacking, so the white man charged at him. Zion quickly pounced out of the corner at the last second, causing the white man to run into the corner of the gate, but he caught himself with his hands.

"You going to make me chase you around this cage all night? Get aggressive with me like you did that Zulu muthafucker!" the white man challenged.

Zion was unfazed. He just continued dancing around the cage, like Muhammad Ali. The white man was obviously a steroid baby, and Zion was smart enough not to go at him head up. He had to use his IQ. "Shut your bitch ass up! I would hit you in your dick, like I did him, but you white, and you full of steroids. That muthafucka probably so little, you won't even feel it."

That seemed to strike a chord in the white man because he charged Zion again, and Zion danced away from him. "You really slow as fuck. I could beat the fuck out of you if I really want to."

The white man waved him in frantically, thick, green veins popping out of his forehead. "Come on, nigger! I'll crush you!"

Zion teased him by coming close and dodging every blow the white man sent his way. He landed a few jabs of his own, but it was nothing crucial. After that, he was back on the run. "I can do this all night. What about you?"

"I'm going to kill you!" the white man spat before faking one way and wrapping his hands around Zion when he tried to dodge him.

He grabbed Zion in a bear hug and lifted him off the ground. Somehow, Zion was able to get his right arm free and came down on top of the white man's head with three fierce elbows to the skull. When his grip loosened a little, Zion wiggled his other arm free and gouged the white man's eyes in with all of his strength.

"Aaaghhhhh!" the white man yelled frantically after dropping Zion and backpedaling into a corner.

Zion made his way in for the kill. The white man must've felt him coming because he started swinging reckless blows that Zion easily dodged. He slipped behind the white man and kicked him down so that he was on his knees. Once he dropped to his knees, Zion was already up on him from behind.

"Time to go meet Hitler, cracker!" he taunted before grabbing his head and snapping his neck forcefully.

Chapter 39

Tory and Big Body went to collect their fortune for the day, and Laney went to go check on her fucking man. Her nerves were shot, and her anxiety was through the roof. There was a locker room in the back, and security granted her access to talk to the fighter, but Lester and Debo had to wait at the entrance.

Laney needed answers because she was lost on so many levels. "Zion, please tell me what the fuck is going on! How did you get out, and why the hell did you agree to fight in this wicked ass tournament? I never seen no shit like this in my whole life. Like what the fuck!"

He sat on the bench, sweaty, as he took swigs from a bottle of Gatorade. "It's a long story. I'll tell you once we get home. I want to take a long, hot bath with you."

"Nah, hell nah!" She shook her head frantically. "I just sat there and watched you literally fight for your life. Not once but twice. You got me fucked up. I need answers right fuckin' now! You had twelve years left on your sentence." She took a seat on the bench to further her point. She needed answers right then.

Zion grabbed his rag and wiped the rest of the blood off of his face. "It's this Russian nigga I was locked up with named Yuteg that's locked up for killing four niggas with his bare hands at a bar. Everybody at the prison was too scared to move in the room with the nigga because he used to beat the fuck out of all his roommates eventually. So, me being me, I move in the room with the nigga my first day at the prison."

"Of course," Laney said while shaking her head disappointedly. "Okay. Keep going. I'm listening."

"So, I'm already onto the nigga because one of the lil' BBG niggas in the dorm put me on point before I went in. After I unpacked all my shit, I called the nigga in the room and locked the door behind him. I could see in his eyes that he was surprised as I threw the first blow, catching him with a quick jab to the chin. We tore that muthafuckin' room up until we both got tired... He told me that was the best fight he had in twenty years. We chopped it up and got cool as fuck after that."

"So, let me guess. He linked you in with the tournament people?" she asked curiously.

"He's one of the original founders of the tournament. I thought the nigga was delusional when he told me about it until he went to showing live fights that were going on all around the world. At first, when he suggested that I participate, I shot him down with the quickness, but as time passed, it started to make sense to me. It started to feel like something I had to do." He took another swig of his drink. "Especially after meeting you. Just made me want to fight for my freedom even more so I finally told Yuteg to set the shit in motion not too long ago. He got his lawyers to work their magic and set up the first tournament in Charlotte. Four weeks later, here we are. I'm a free and rich man now... I want the future we're going to build together bad as hell. That's what I was out there fighting for."

"I love your crazy ass to death... I can see why you kept all this shit away from me but damnnnn, nigga! You just gave a bitch two whole heart attacks. What if you didn't make it up out of that cage, Zion? What the fuck was I supposed to do? How could I move on from that?" she asked with a single tear rolling down her face.

He looked over at her, and he allowed himself to soften up immediately. He scooted closer and pulled her into his arms. "I know you wouldn't be able to. That's why I made sure you ain't have to. Fuck what would've and could've been. I'm here now, in the flesh, and we got the rest of our lives ahead of us."

Laney couldn't hold the tears in any longer. She just hugged him tightly and let her tears flow with her face buried in his chest. It felt so good to finally be in his embrace. She'd dreamed of his return to the streets a million different times before and never imagined it being like this. Either way it went, she had him in her arms, and she planned on never letting go.

TO BE CONTINUED...

Lock Down Publications and Ca$h Presents
Assisted Publishing Packages

BASIC PACKAGE $499 Editing Cover Design Formatting	UPGRADED PACKAGE $800 Typing Editing Cover Design Formatting
ADVANCE PACKAGE $1,200 Typing Editing Cover Design Formatting Copyright registration Proofreading Upload book to Amazon	LDP SUPREME PACKAGE $1,500 Typing Editing Cover Design Formatting Copyright registration Proofreading Set up Amazon account Upload book to Amazon Advertise on LDP, Amazon and Facebook Page

***Other services available upon request.
Additional charges may apply

Lock Down Publications
P.O. Box 944
Stockbridge, GA 30281-9998
Phone: 470 303-9761

Submission Guideline

Submit the first three chapters of your completed manuscript to ldpsubmissions@gmail.com. In the subject line add **Your Book's Title**. The manuscript must be in a Word Doc file and sent as an attachment. Document should be in Times New Roman, double spaced, and in size 12 font. Also, provide your synopsis and full contact information. If sending multiple submissions, they must each be in a separate email.

Have a story but no way to send it electronically? You can still submit to LDP/Ca$h Presents. Send in the first three chapters, written or typed, of your completed manuscript to:

LDP: Submissions Dept
P.O. Box 944
Stockbridge, GA 30281-9998

DO NOT send original manuscript. Must be a duplicate.
Provide your synopsis and a cover letter containing your full contact information.

Thanks for considering LDP and Ca$h Presents.

NEW RELEASES

BLOODLINE OF A SAVAGE 1&2
THESE VICIOUS STREETS
RELENTLESS GOON
RELENTLESS GOON 2
BY PRINCE A. TAUHID

THE BUTTERFLY MAFIA 1-3
BY FUMIYA PAYNE

A THUG'S STREET PRINCESS 1&2
BY MEESHA

CITY OF SMOKE 2
BY MOLOTTI

STEPPERS 1,2&3
BY KING RIO

THE LANE 1&2
BY KEN-KEN SPENCE

THUG OF SPADES 1&2
LOVE IN THE TRENCHES 2
BY COREY ROBINSON

TIL DEATH 3
BY ARYANNA

THE BIRTH OF A GANGSTER 4
BY DELMONT PLAYER

PRODUCT OF THE STREETS 1&2
BY DEMOND "MONEY" ANDERSON

NO TIME FOR ERROR
BY KEESE

MONEY HUNGRY DEMONS
BY TRANAY ADAMS

Coming Soon from Lock Down Publications/Ca$h Presents

IF YOU CROSS ME ONCE 6
ANGEL V
By Anthony Fields

IMMA DIE BOUT MINE 4&5
By Aryanna

A THUGS STREET PRINCESS 3
By Meesha

PRODUCT OF THE STREETS 3
By Demond Money Anderson

CORNER BOYS
By Corey Robinson

SON OF A DOPE FIEND 4
By Renta

THE MURDER QUEENS 6&7
By Michael Gallon

CITY OF SMOKE 3
By Molotti

BETRAYAL OF A G
By Ray Vinci

CONFESSIONS OF A DOPE BOY
By Nicholas Lock

THA TAKEOVER
By Keith Chandler

Available Now

RESTRAINING ORDER 1 & 2
By **CA$H & Coffee**

LOVE KNOWS NO BOUNDARIES 1-3
By **Coffee**

RAISED AS A GOON I, II, III & IV
BRED BY THE SLUMS I, II, III
BLAST FOR ME I & II
ROTTEN TO THE CORE I II III
A BRONX TALE I, II, III
DUFFLE BAG CARTEL I II III IV V VI
HEARTLESS GOON I II III IV V
A SAVAGE DOPEBOY I II
DRUG LORDS I II III
CUTTHROAT MAFIA I II
KING OF THE TRENCHES
By **Ghost**

LAY IT DOWN I & II
LAST OF A DYING BREED I II
BLOOD STAINS OF A SHOTTA I & II III
By **Jamaica**

LOYAL TO THE GAME I II III
LIFE OF SIN I, II III
By **TJ & Jelissa**

IF LOVING HIM IS WRONG…I & II
LOVE ME EVEN WHEN IT HURTS I II III
By **Jelissa**

BLOODY COMMAS I & II
SKI MASK CARTEL I, II & III
KING OF NEW YORK I II, III IV V
RISE TO POWER I II III
COKE KINGS I II III IV V
BORN HEARTLESS I II III IV
KING OF THE TRAP I II
By **T.J. Edwards**

WHEN THE STREETS CLAP BACK I & II III
THE HEART OF A SAVAGE I II III IV
MONEY MAFIA I II
LOYAL TO THE SOIL I II III
By **Jibril Williams**

A DISTINGUISHED THUG STOLE MY HEART I II &
III
LOVE SHOULDN'T HURT I II III IV
RENEGADE BOYS 1-4
PAID IN KARMA 1-3
SAVAGE STORMS 1-3
AN UNFORESEEN LOVE 1-3
BABY, I'M WINTERTIME COLD 1-3
A THUG'S STREET PRINCESS 1&2
By **Meesha**

A GANGSTER'S CODE 1-3
A GANGSTER'S SYN 1-3
THE SAVAGE LIFE 1-3
CHAINED TO THE STREETS 1-3
BLOOD ON THE MONEY 1-3
A GANGSTA'S PAIN 1-3
BEAUTIFUL LIES AND UGLY TRUTHS
CHURCH IN THESE STREETS
By **J-Blunt**

PUSH IT TO THE LIMIT
By **Bre' Hayes**

BLOOD OF A BOSS 1-5
SHADOWS OF THE GAME
TRAP BASTARD
By **Askari**

THE STREETS BLEED MURDER 1-3
THE HEART OF A GANGSTA 1-3
By **Jerry Jackson**

CUM FOR ME 1-8
An LDP Erotica Collaboration

BRIDE OF A HUSTLA 1-3
THE FETTI GIRLS 1-3
CORRUPTED BY A GANGSTA 1-4
BLINDED BY HIS LOVE
THE PRICE YOU PAY FOR LOVE 1-3
DOPE GIRL MAGIC 1-3
By **Destiny Skai**

WHEN A GOOD GIRL GOES BAD
By **Adrienne**

A KINGPIN'S AMBITION
A KINGPIN'S AMBITION II
I MURDER FOR THE DOUGH
By **Ambitious**

THE COST OF LOYALTY 1-3
By **Kweli**

A GANGSTER'S REVENGE 1-4
THE BOSS MAN'S DAUGHTERS 1-5
A SAVAGE LOVE 1&2
BAE BELONGS TO ME 1&2
A HUSTLER'S DECEIT 1-3
WHAT BAD BITCHES DO 1-3
SOUL OF A MONSTER 1-3
KILL ZONE
A DOPE BOY'S QUEEN 1-3
TIL DEATH 1-3
IMMA DIE BOUT MINE 1-3
By **Aryanna**

TRUE SAVAGE 1-7
DOPE BOY MAGIC 1-3
MIDNIGHT CARTEL 1-3
CITY OF KINGZ 1&2
NIGHTMARE ON SILENT AVE
THE PLUG OF LIL MEXICO 1&2
CLASSIC CITY
By **Chris Green**

A DOPEBOY'S PRAYER
By **Eddie "Wolf" Lee**

THE KING CARTEL 1-3
By **Frank Gresham**

THESE NIGGAS AIN'T LOYAL 1-3
By **Nikki Tee**

GANGSTA SHYT 1-3
By **CATO**

THE ULTIMATE BETRAYAL
By **Phoenix**

BOSS'N UP 1-3
By **Royal Nicole**

I LOVE YOU TO DEATH
By **Destiny J**

I RIDE FOR MY HITTA
I STILL RIDE FOR MY HITTA
By **Misty Holt**

LOVE & CHASIN' PAPER
By **Qay Crockett**

TO DIE IN VAIN
SINS OF A HUSTLA
By **ASAD**

BROOKLYN HUSTLAZ
By **Boogsy Morina**

BROOKLYN ON LOCK 1 & 2
By **Sonovia**

GANGSTA CITY
By T**eddy Duke**

A DRUG KING AND HIS DIAMOND 1-3
A DOPEMAN'S RICHES
HER MAN, MINE'S TOO 1&2
CASH MONEY HO'S
THE WIFEY I USED TO BE 1&2
PRETTY GIRLS DO NASTY THINGS
By **Nicole Goosby**

LIPSTICK KILLAH 1-3
CRIME OF PASSION 1-3
FRIEND OR FOE 1-3
By **Mimi**

TRAPHOUSE KING 1-3
KINGPIN KILLAZ 1-3
STREET KINGS 1&2
PAID IN BLOOD 1&2
CARTEL KILLAZ 1-3
DOPE GODS 1&2
By **Hood Rich**

STEADY MOBBN' 1-3
THE STREETS STAINED MY SOUL 1-3
By **Marcellus Allen**

WHO SHOT YA 1-3
SON OF A DOPE FIEND 1-3
HEAVEN GOT A GHETTO 1&2
SKI MASK MONEY 1&2
By **Renta**

GORILLAZ IN THE BAY 1-4
TEARS OF A GANGSTA 1/&2
3X KRAZY 1&2
STRAIGHT BEAST MODE 1&2
By **DE'KARI**

TRIGGADALE 1-3
MURDA WAS THE CASE 1-3
By **Elijah R. Freeman**

THE STREETS ARE CALLING
By **Duquie Wilson**

SLAUGHTER GANG 1-3
RUTHLESS HEART 1-3
By **Willie Slaughter**

GOD BLESS THE TRAPPERS 1-3
THESE SCANDALOUS STREETS 1-3
FEAR MY GANGSTA 1-5
THESE STREETS DON'T LOVE NOBODY 1-2
BURY ME A G 1-5
A GANGSTA'S EMPIRE 1-4
THE DOPEMAN'S BODYGAURD 1&2
THE REALEST KILLAZ 1-3
THE LAST OF THE OGS 1-3
By **Tranay Adams**

MARRIED TO A BOSS 1-3
By **Destiny Skai & Chris Green**

KINGZ OF THE GAME 1-7
CRIME BOSS 1-3
By **Playa Ray**

FUK SHYT
By **Blakk Diamond**

DON'T F#CK WITH MY HEART 1&2
By **Linnea**

ADDICTED TO THE DRAMA 1-3
IN THE ARM OF HIS BOSS
By **Jamila**

LOYALTY AIN'T PROMISED 1&2
By **Keith Williams**

YAYO 1-4
A SHOOTER'S AMBITION 1&2
BRED IN THE GAME
By **S. Allen**

TRAP GOD 1-3
RICH $AVAGE 1-3
MONEY IN THE GRAVE 1-3
CARTEL MONEY
By **Martell Troublesome Bolden**

FOREVER GANGSTA 1&2
GLOCKS ON SATIN SHEETS 1&2
By **Adrian Dulan**

TOE TAGZ 1-4
LEVELS TO THIS SHYT 1&2
IT'S JUST ME AND YOU
By **Ah'Million**

KINGPIN DREAMS 1-3
RAN OFF ON DA PLUG
By **Paper Boi Rari**

CONFESSIONS OF A GANGSTA 1-4
CONFESSIONS OF A JACKBOY 1-3
CONFESSIONS OF A HITMAN
By **Nicholas Lock**

I'M NOTHING WITHOUT HIS LOVE
SINS OF A THUG
TO THE THUG I LOVED BEFORE
A GANGSTA SAVED XMAS
IN A HUSTLER I TRUST
By **Monet Dragun**

QUIET MONEY 1-3
THUG LIFE 1-3
EXTENDED CLIP 1&2
A GANGSTA'S PARADISE
By **Trai'Quan**

CAUGHT UP IN THE LIFE 1-3
THE STREETS NEVER LET GO 1-3
By **Robert Baptiste**

NEW TO THE GAME 1-3
MONEY, MURDER & MEMORIES 1-3
By **Malik D. Rice**

CREAM 2-3
THE STREETS WILL TALK
By **Yolanda Moore**

LIFE OF A SAVAGE 1-4
A GANGSTA'S QUR'AN 1-4
MURDA SEASON 1-3
GANGLAND CARTEL 1-3
CHI'RAQ GANGSTAS 1-4
KILLERS ON ELM STREET 1-3
JACK BOYZ N DA BRONX 1-3
A DOPEBOY'S DREAM 1-3
JACK BOYS VS DOPE BOYS 1-3
COKE GIRLZ
COKE BOYS
SOSA GANG 1&2
BRONX SAVAGES
BODYMORE KINGPINS
BLOOD OF A GOON
By **Romell Tukes**

THE STREETS MADE ME 1-3
By **Larry D. Wright**

CONCRETE KILLA 1-3
VICIOUS LOYALTY 1-3
By **Kingpen**

THE ULTIMATE SACRIFICE 1-6
KHADIFI
IF YOU CROSS ME ONCE 1-3
ANGEL 1-4
IN THE BLINK OF AN EYE
By **Anthony Fields**

THE LIFE OF A HOOD STAR
By **Ca$h & Rashia Wilson**

THE STREETS WILL NEVER CLOSE 1-3
By **K'ajji**

NIGHTMARES OF A HUSTLA 1-3
By **King Dream**

HARD AND RUTHLESS 1&2
MOB TOWN 251
THE BILLIONAIRE BENTLEYS 1-3
REAL G'S MOVE IN SILENCE
By **Von Diesel**

GHOST MOB
By **Stilloan Robinson**

MOB TIES 1-6
SOUL OF A HUSTLER, HEART OF A KILLER 1-3
GORILLAZ IN THE TRENCHES
By **SayNoMore**

BODYMORE MURDERLAND 1-3
THE BIRTH OF A GANGSTER 1-4
By **Delmont Player**

FOR THE LOVE OF A BOSS 1&2
By **C. D. Blue**

KILLA KOUNTY 1-5
By **Khufu**

MOBBED UP 1-4
THE BRICK MAN 1-5
THE COCAINE PRINCESS 1-10
STEPPERS 1-3
SUPER GREMLIN 1-4
By **King Rio**

MONEY GAME 1&2
By **Smoove Dolla**

A GANGSTA'S KARMA 1-4
By **FLAME**

KING OF THE TRENCHES 1-3
By **GHOST & TRANAY ADAMS**

QUEEN OF THE ZOO 1&2
By **Black Migo**

GRIMEY WAYS 1-3
By **Ray Vinci**

XMAS WITH AN ATL SHOOTER
By **Ca$h & Destiny Skai**

KING KILLA 1&2
By **Vincent "Vitto" Holloway**

BETRAYAL OF A THUG 1&2
By **Fre$h**

THE MURDER QUEENS 1-5
By **Michael Gallon**

FOR THE LOVE OF BLOOD 1-4
By **Jamel Mitchell**

HOOD CONSIGLIERE 1&2
NO TIME FOR ERROR
By **Keese**

PROTÉGÉ OF A LEGEND 1&2
LOVE IN THE TRENCHES 1&2
By **Corey Robinson**

BORN IN THE GRAVE 1-3
CRIME PAYS
By **Self Made Tay**

MOAN IN MY MOUTH
By **XTASY**

TORN BETWEEN A GANGSTER AND A GENTLEMAN
By **J-BLUNT & Miss Kim**

LOYALTY IS EVERYTHING 1-3
CITY OF SMOKE 1&2
By **Molotti**

HERE TODAY GONE TOMORROW 1&2
By **Fly Rock**

WOMEN LIE MEN LIE 1-4
FIFTY SHADES OF SNOW 1-3
STACK BEFORE YOU SPLURGE
GIRLS FALL LIKE DOMINOES
NAÏVE TO THE STREETS
By **ROY MILLIGAN**

PILLOW PRINCESS
By **S. Hawkins**

THE BUTTERFLY MAFIA 1-3
SALUTE MY SAVAGERY 1&2
By **Fumiya Payne**

THE LANE 1&2
By Ken-Ken Spence

THE PUSSY TRAP 1-5
By **Nene Capri**

DIRTY DNA
By **Blaque**

SANCTIFIED AND HORNY
by **XTASY**

BOOKS BY LDP'S CEO, CA$H

TRUST IN NO MAN
TRUST IN NO MAN 2
TRUST IN NO MAN 3
BONDED BY BLOOD
SHORTY GOT A THUG
THUGS CRY
THUGS CRY 2
THUGS CRY 3
TRUST NO BITCH
TRUST NO BITCH 2
TRUST NO BITCH 3
TIL MY CASKET DROPS
RESTRAINING ORDER
RESTRAINING ORDER 2
IN LOVE WITH A CONVICT
LIFE OF A HOOD STAR
XMAS WITH AN ATL SHOOTER

www.ingramcontent.com/pod-product-compliance
Lightning Source LLC
Chambersburg PA
CBHW070521260626
47161CB00004B/1606